# UNICORN
# SISTERS

## URSULA HOLDEN

Methuen

First published in Great Britain 1988
by Methuen London Ltd
11 New Fetter Lane, London EC4P 4EE

British Library Cataloguing in Publication Data

Holden, Ursula
   Unicorn sisters.
   I. Title
   823'.914[F]      PR6058.0434

   ISBN 0–413–16640–6

Printed and bound in Great Britain
by Redwood Burn Ltd,
Trowbridge, Wiltshire

For my daughters

# ONE

'You'll miss me, darlings, I know you will. I know I'll miss you, too.'

Once Mamma had decided to leave us again she kept repeating this, like the refrain of a song or a prayer. She said we must be brave soldiers, she knew what was best for us. The three of us were to go to a boarding school, a place of safety, out of reach of Hitler's bombs. She hugged me and my two sisters, leaving wafts of perfume in our hair. She touched our hands which embarrassed us, we were not used to the touch of adults. We were used to her being away.

I loved the soft feel of her fur jacket, the feeling of fur against my face. She wore her collar turned up to frame her cheeks and hair. When she was at home I used to listen for the tap of her coloured heels, the swish of petticoats. She was perfect.

She had red hair that September when war was declared but sometimes it was just mouse brown. Mamma was relieved to be getting rid of us so conveniently. War was declared. We must go at once.

She was stage struck; we were used to her going away to her acting. This time we were leaving her because of the present emergency.

'And, Bonnie, darling, I leave you in charge. Promise me you will take care of your sisters. They will feel strange at first, at school.'

Her hair clung beguilingly to her fur collar. While we were safely in the West Country she planned to sing and act for the troops. She would join a company, tour the country to make the army smile.

So then, it was settled, she would miss and think of us constantly. She had discovered the perfect school where we could stay in the holidays as well as the term, a school which catered for girls with absent parents. We only had Mamma, our father was already dead. Entertaining the forces would be Mamma's war effort, more valuable than fighting with guns. There was no question of us staying with her. She needed to be free.

'It's a charming place, run by two sisters. I've seen the prospectus. They cater for girls from six to sixteen. So, Bonnie, you'll be substitute mother, won't you?'

She widened her lashes, her beautiful eyes appealed. 'Bonnie, darling, I shall miss you. You're my right hand, my aide-de-camp.'

I looked away. I didn't want to co-operate. I wanted her to stay. In wartime children needed parents more than ever, not just because of bombs but because everything had changed. We didn't want to go to strange teachers in a strange school in a strange county. Why should I act as a mother when I was their sister? I needed her, so did Ula and Tor.

The three of us had been in Ireland earlier, for a holiday. Home had seemed far away. When we got back there were soldiers everywhere, on motor bikes, in lorries, peering from the tops of tanks. The atmosphere felt hectic, with housewives wondering and worrying about soap and biscuits and other household articles that might become in short supply. There were first aid courses at the Town

Hall, there were gas masks to be collected. You needed air-raid shelters to keep you safe from raids. But the soldiers looked carefree, shouting at girls to make them giggle, revving motor cycles and whistling. The girls nudged each other, the wailing notes of the whistles made them blush and comb their hair after the soldiers had passed. I couldn't imagine anyone wanting to whistle at me.

Mamma had letters and telephone calls that made her anxious. The War Office wanted to requisition our home. When we left it soldiers would move in and live here. A regiment was stationed in our town. The War Office would pay Mamma for the use of our house; a help, she said, towards the fees of our school. While we studied in the West Country Mamma would be singing for soldiers, uplifting their morale. She would stay with the others in her company, we must not worry about her safety. She knew that we would love our school. Our uniform was only to be obtained at Liberty's. Imagine, darlings. And we must be fitted with gas masks too.

A man with ARP on his shoulder put rubber masks on our faces and made us breathe while he checked for a correct fit. The rubber had a choking smell like cooking stoves which I hated, but Ula was thrilled. They were kept in cardboard boxes with string handles, they must be carried at all times. Notices read: 'Have you got your gas mask?' Mamma thought they were deplorable; they messed your hair and spoiled your skin. When she was singing for the army she might get a better one with long breathing tubes like the soldiers. Ula patted and examined hers, swinging it with pride. Tor didn't say what she thought, she never did. I could usually guess what she was thinking, she and I were so close.

The day after we got our gas masks we went to London for the uniform. We were quite vague about why the country was at war, we only knew it made a lot of changes.

9

We walked through the revolving doors of Liberty's. Ula showing off with her gas mask. I already felt responsible for my sisters because I'd been put in charge. Soon we were in our vests and knickers, trying on uniforms. I had made Tor and Ula leave off their bodices, in case they were laughed at in the shop but the assistant was motherly. Until now no one had bothered about our clothes; we wore ugly skirts and grey jerseys. Now the fitting room became piled with tunics and blouses that gave off that special wool smell. Mamma, smelling of attar of roses, sat smiling and watching us change; the perfect fond mother kitting out her daughters.

The uniform was a light rust colour with contrasting tomato red or coral pink. Our blouses were tussore silk, our underwear Chilprufe, our velour hats had rust-coloured turned-back brims. I never dreamed that I would own so many lovely clothes. Our feet danced as we left the school outfitting floor. We were like three princesses dressed extravagantly for an unknown future ball.

On the ground floor Mamma paused at the perfume counter to replenish her essences and her beautiful rose-smelling soaps. When she sang the soldiers would be able to smell as well as see and hear her. She sprayed the air round my face. 'Lovely isn't it, my sweet Bonnie? How I'll miss you.' The assistants watched and whispered. What lucky children. What a lovely mamma.

We went to a restaurant where a three-piece band was playing. Romantic tunes accompanied our tinkling spoons. Mamma hummed in a throaty way; she never tired of that song, she said.

'Sing the words, Mamma.'

'When I grow too old to dream, I'll have you to remember. When I grow too old to dream, your love will live in my heart.'

She sang too loudly, but I liked it. I watched her biting into a sandwich, looking lively and exotic. Her real world awaited her, her world of cocktail parties where people discussed love affairs and gossiped about stars of film and stage.

'I love cream cakes,' Ula said, reaching for another.

'Sweet child, don't make yourself sick, will you? You're not in Ireland now.'

Ula choked. She asked why we had to go so far away.

'The bombs, darling. Hitler is the culprit. You must be educated. It's unfortunate, I know. You have your sisters. Bonnie has promised to look after you.'

'Do I have a choice?' I muttered. But the school uniform was worth the bother and upheaval of war.

The London streets were crowded with soldiers in their best uniforms, off duty now, their guns and packs put away. With boots and buttons glistening, they had their loved ones, and money to spend. Those without a girl looked lost and lonely, standing at corners and waiting, or bunched in groups looking at maps. Freedom was sweet.

At the next table an officer had sat with his fiancée. With chairs touching, they had eyes for nothing but themselves and their diamond ring. They hadn't noticed when Mamma had sung.

Sandbags were piled in front of windows to protect them from shattering. Underground exits had boardings to protect travellers from blast. There were crash barriers where crowds might gather. Above our heads the barrage balloons floated in the clouds, like huge, unlikely-looking whales. There were posters everywhere urging and encouraging: 'Dig for Victory', 'Careless Talk Costs Lives'. Ula wanted to know what 'Save for the Brave and Lend to Defend the Right to be Free' meant. She couldn't read yet. Tor read the slogans aloud. Mamma said that it was a good thing to stock up on perfumes, anything might become rationed in wartime. Now that I had my uniform I had no interest in the war or rationing. I would miss

11

Mamma but I still had Tor. We had never been apart. We had shared our schoolroom and had been taught by an old governess. Mamma was like a remote perfumed butterfly; when she alit you longed to keep her. I could only guess at her real world that she liked best.

'I'd like to wear a tin helmet,' Ula said. 'I'd like to be an ARP man.'

'We must all make sacrifices for our country,' Mamma said, looking dreamily at her rings. The couple at the next table had kissed their ring before kissing each other. Mamma's rings were glittery and precious, put on her fingers long ago by Papa. Soon she would be telling us that she would miss us for the last time. We would smell roses, feel her hands on our hands. She'd be gone. I decided to wear the velvet collar of my tweed coat turned up like hers. I would experiment with the brim of my hat. The school was called Magnolia House. The headmistress was called Miss Gee.

'I love school,' Ula said.

'How do you know? You haven't tried it. Don't be so sure.'

'Not long now. Hurry, my darlings, or we'll miss the six o'clock train home.'

And then it was the first day of term and we were driving to the West Country. It was a low building behind a white wall, the autumn evening was damp with fog in patches. On the school gatepost was a small unicorn.

'And look Bonnie, they've got a magnolia tree.' Mamma sounded nervous now. We looked at the knobbly branches growing in a tangle in front of the conservatory to the right of the front door. There were no plants on the front lawn, no autumn daisies or chrysanthemums, just grass and the wet grey branches of the tree.

'I like the unicorn,' Ula said in a small voice.

'It's so quiet. Where are all the girls, Mamma?'

'Children, darlings. This is where I leave you. We'll part

12

here, I won't come in. Look, your headmistress is at the window.'

We saw a thin person behind the magnolia branches standing in the conservatory.

'Stay, Mamma. Don't go yet.'

'Don't linger, darlings. Go in. Kiss me. Quick.'

'Mamma. ...'

Remember the feel of her hair on your cheek, her perfume, her wide open eyes. Remember the rings on her white fingers, put there by Papa long ago. You mustn't go yet, Mamma, you must meet Miss Gee, you must talk to her. I have never met or spoken to a teacher. I don't know what to say.

'Bona? What a tall girl. You must be the eldest. But why did your mother not wait? How strange.'

'She's very busy. It's her war work, you know,' Ula explained.

Miss Gee moved stiffly back through the white doorway. She hadn't smiled, her face was thin and stern. Her clothes, her skin and hair were a pale greyish shade. She spoke through half-closed lips. She closed the door. We were cut off from Mamma. We heard the taxi drive off. We are alone now with Miss Gee.

Her study was severe, with just a desk and a cupboard for her files. Mamma had left without seeing our bedrooms or the rooms where we would work and eat. Did she even know what we would be learning?

Tor and I could read anything. We had learned from the same books that Mamma had used, because Gov had once taught her too. They were mildewed and had broken spines mended with brown paper. When you turned the page you got a smell of church. We had learned no maths or geography or languages. Ula had done no lessons at all apart from Tor teaching her letters. We used to keep her out of the schoolroom, it was our private domain. No wonder she looked forward to being with us. Ula wasn't afraid of anyone, not even Miss Gee now. She reminded me of a knight on a tombstone, stony-faced and grim.

She wrote our names in her register. She asked about our health. Had we had measles, chicken-pox, mumps?

'I don't think we ever had any illnesses.'

Not having mixed with other children we hadn't caught their germs. When we were little we had gone to a dancing class. Our health was good because we had stayed at home with our governess. A lump came into my throat when I thought of her. She had been deaf and she'd slept a lot but was good-humoured and fond of us.

'Except for our brother, Bonnie. Don't forget about him. He died of croup.'

'*Ula*.'

I hated her for mentioning our brother. Having no father and a mother who ran off without waiting was bad enough. Whatever would Miss Gee think of us?

She didn't answer but went on writing. When she looked up her eyes were cold and sad. Was there any food that didn't agree with us? Nothing? Very well. We were to sleep together in the larger dormitory. The smaller one was not at present in use. The school, she explained, was not operating at full capacity. Owing to the war the pupil quota had been reduced. The term did not start until tomorrow. Why our mother had seen fit to leave us a day early was a mystery. The other pupils would arrive tomorrow, the official start of term. What a pity that our mother had not stayed a moment, had not troubled to make herself known.

'We thought we had to come today. Mamma must have made a mistake.'

'A pity. I like to interview new parents.'

'Our mamma is going to sing for the army. The war is going to move into our home. I like your school, Miss Gee. I see you have that message "Save for the Brave". We saw it in London.'

The slogan was printed on the lid of a cash box on the windowsill. I explained that Ula was excited, that she wasn't used to school. She was naturally talkative. Miss Gee mustn't know that she couldn't read or that Tor and I knew no algebra or French. Ula could remember the shapes of words once she'd been told what they said. If only Mamma had talked to Miss Gee. If only we hadn't come a day too soon. She continued writing without answering. She wrote with a steel nib dipped into an ink-well. She blotted her copperplate writing with clean blotting paper. Now, new girls. Come with her. I wished she would smile.

I wished that Mamma had seen the drab dormitory with the faded curtains that separated the beds. The ceiling was cracked like a piece of china. Upstairs was much shabbier than below. Perhaps parents were not encouraged up here. Mamma never had concerned herself about our education or our activities. We had never been taught religion. At this school it seemed to be important, there was a chapel room downstairs.

'If a bomb fell that ceiling might fall on us, Miss Gee.'

Miss Gee didn't answer Ula. She went downstairs.

'Don't talk so much, Ula. It's best to keep quiet until we know the ropes.'

Tomorrow eleven girls would arrive. Fourteen pupils was not a large school, more a group than an establishment. I looked down the dormitory with the double row of waiting beds. I stroked the tussore silk sleeve of my blouse. I had fawn silk stockings for Sundays, I had brown strap shoes with little heels. When we had looked into the chapel room Miss Gee's face had gone gentle. The school assembled there every morning, it was the focus of the school day. She had said that the girls were encouraged to be self-governing, school was but a training for life. An old gardener had carried our suitcases up, they were waiting beside our beds. The grey curtains hung from metal poles

15

by rings. They clattered when you gave a pull.

'Don't break them, Ula. Take care.'

The window curtains were lined with black cotton to comply with black-out rules. Enemy aircraft could attack at night, not a chink of light must show. Every street light, every traffic light and car light must be dimmed now because of war. We would feel better when we had unpacked our clothes. I would put Mamma and the war out of my mind as I unfolded new sweaters and vests. I would gloat again over my tussore silks and tweeds. Even our hankies were pastel coloured; we were like three pink and rust butterfly brides. We moved from our suitcases to our beds, sorting and piling. I helped Ula to refold her skirts. She worried and annoyed me constantly with her high spirits and thoughtless remarks. She had stayed in Ireland for longer than Tor and me. Before we got there a dreadful thing had happened to Ula which cast a black shadow over our lives. She had accidentally caused the death of her friend Lucy and we never spoke about it. Ula hadn't shown any grief but it would probably affect her always. It had happened soon after the death of our brother Bruno and we rarely spoke about him either. Probably this war would affect us all deeply, though Mamma was too old to change.

The responsibility fell on me, I would keep my promise. Ula was wriggling over the bedrails like a snake, crumpling her clothes again.

'I'll sleep in the middle, shall I, Bonnie?'

'No you won't, thanks very much. Tor and I stay together.'

Ula stared with her silly smile. She had a freak streak of white hair over her forehead which stuck up sometimes like a little horn. If only she were not so noticeable and talkative. We all had rather poor-coloured teeth but I was the prettiest and the one most fond of clothes. Ula started wrapping a pink hankie round her gas mask, rocking and kissing it like a child. She never took offence, was always cheerful. Tor hardly spoke at all. I knew and understood her, she liked to read and keep a diary. Both were even-tempered and never spiteful, I knew their good qualities too.

At the end of the dormitory was a row of wash-basins that you tipped into a drain behind. They were thick and clumsy, too heavy for Ula. I watched her struggling. Tor went to her help. The water swished. We heard it gurgle; the plumbing seemed to be old. We sat on our beds and looked at our clothes again. There were no carpets anywhere.

When we had put everything into the chests of drawers we went downstairs again. We felt hungry.

There were long tables in the dining room. Miss Gee had made the tea herself because we had come early. After today there would be just a light supper at night.

'What's in this sandwich, Miss Gee? I like it.'

She told Ula that it was called Patum Peperium, made from anchovies, which some called Gentlemen's Relish. She hadn't smiled yet. Did she pity us or despise us for having dead or neglectful parents? She didn't speak any more but kept her eyes on a list of names. As well as fewer pupils she seemed to have a servant problem, another result of this war. The dining room smelled of old frying pans. Ula was greedy about the sandwiches. I was deeply ashamed to see her wiping her mouth on a lock of her hair.

'It isn't dark yet, Miss Gee. Can I go and look at that unicorn again?'

Miss Gee said that the front of the school was out of bounds without an adult, no girl was to go near the gate. There were few rules, that was one of them; do not go near the gate. We might put on our Wellington boots if we wished and walk round the croquet lawn but stick to the paths, please.

17

Our Wellingtons were brown. The label said 'Made in France'. So far the nicest part of coming here was the clothing. Mamma had spent a lot, she must care about us. The boots squeaked as our ankles brushed together. They made slushing sounds in the wet leaves. The twilight air was bitter against our faces, we felt too awed and nervous to jump or run. At home we used to love kicking autumn leaves or catching them as they fell. The croquet hoops made crooked loops against the cold no-coloured grass. Ula pushed her boot into one of them. 'Look, Bonnie. I'm an animal in a trap.'

'Get off the grass. The lawn is only for teachers. You heard what Miss Gee said.'

'What teachers? I haven't seen any except her. Look, a mole has been here, look at that mound over there.'

'Do get off. It's not allowed.'

'I want to see the unicorn. I must.'

'You heard. No.'

But I wanted to see it too. Even more, I wanted to hear cars passing. We were cut off and silent here, with only the slush of leaves and the squeaking of our boots. By now Mamma would be home again. Was she thinking of us while she sipped her evening cocktail? A lot seemed to be expected of me. Miss Gee had said that she liked those with long hair to wear it plaited. Ula's wasn't long enough, Tor wore hers quite short and straight. I hated plaits. There would be no supper tonight. Come back, Ula, you are not to go in the front.

I ran round the side of the building after her. She was standing by the magnolia tree looking at the unicorn. It was difficult to see now in the dying light, just a small lump on the gatepost with a horn sticking out. The magnolia tree was a blur.

'You must do what I say, Ula. You've got to learn.'

I put my hand out and pinched her, that would teach her. She clutched her neck. 'That hurt, Bonnie. Don't.'

18

I had never hurt her physically before and I felt ashamed and sorry. She was only young after all, she couldn't help having accidentally killed someone, she couldn't help her irritating ways. I resolved never to hit or hurt either of them while I was their guardian, I would love them and keep them from harm. 'I'm sorry, Ula, honestly.'

'Oh, all right. Is that a rat or a rabbit over there?'

'It's just leaves, you fool. Come on.'

We had to use a torch in the bathroom that separated the large and the small dormitories, there were no black-out curtains there yet. The three baths were divided by wooden partitions that you could see over if you climbed them. We could listen to each other splashing peacefully. Miss Gee had told us to use separate baths. Modesty remained a virtue despite war. She gave me a torch. I must keep this pointed low; remember no light must be visible from the sky. As important as modesty and the conceal-ment of light was the saving of hot water. The level must not rise above the mark painted round the bathtub. Fuel was needed for the war effort. 'Save for the Brave and Lend to Defend the Right to be Free.' And please draw the cubicle curtains when dressing and undressing.

I aimed the torch under the partition. I could see Tor's bony little feet. Each cubicle had a slatted mat to step on to. There was a wooden rack for your sponge. Ula whispered that there might be spiders. Tor said that cock-roaches were more likely. She had hardly spoken since we got here. At home we used to collect spiders, not having other pets. They always died. If I hadn't felt so responsible and homesick I might have enjoyed the bath. Faint starlight shone through the window. Was it dark enough for a raid? I heard my sisters' watery sounds, I heard Tor drop her shoe. Ula liked practising whistling in the bath; she hadn't learned it yet. Water was supposed to improve sound. Tor was finished first. I loved and understood Tor

19

better than anyone, we never quarrelled or got bored. There was no need for anyone else when we were together, but I wished we'd bought something to read in bed. I stared into the starry blackness and imagined a castle made of roses, snow and moonlight for us to live in. I supposed we'd have to let Ula in too.

'Hurry then, Ula. We're getting into bed now.'

Mamma had given each of us a tube of face cream. The water at school might be hard. The West Country wasn't mild like the south, the winds might roughen our skins. Nightly creaming ensured good looks later, use it, darling, don't forget. We sat up in bed spreading the cream diligently, not forgetting our necks. We patted it round our eyes. The cream was made in France like our Wellingtons, it shone pure and shiny white. Ula gasped; she'd been using her toothpaste. 'It's all pepperminty. It stings, Bonnie, what shall I do?'

'You might get a disease. Wash it off quickly, Ula.'

She made a lot of noise heaving and banging the washbasin. Tor went to her help again.

In the night Ula made more noises, groaning and grinding her teeth together. She often did this at home since the accident in Ireland. I shook her shoulder. She had her gas mask under the sheet with her. She looked so innocent and startled. I must never hurt her again.

'You must try and sleep quietly. You must learn to fit in. The girls won't like you to be different. You must try and get your own friends and do what I say.'

# TWO

I woke early. Today was the real start of the Christmas term. Soon we would see the other girls. They would know each other, they would know the staff and the timetable. I worried for my sisters' sake the most. I put my hand to the heating pipes above my head. I guessed they'd be almost cold. The black curtains fitted the windows without any light showing. At home Mamma would be snuggling into her pillows, pulling up her eiderdown. Her life would soon change too. When your country needed your services, you were told what to do, you obeyed. Some people liked being instructed, liked being fitted with gas masks and planning shelters for raids, liked growing vegetables and saving fuel. Mamma would like singing to soldiers while she left her family to me. I hoped we wouldn't be laughed at for being backward, for having no father and rather poor teeth. The uniform was my mainstay and comfort, even my pyjamas were new; soft pink and rose coloured stripes. My face cream was like a talisman, smelling a little like Mamma's rosy scent. There was no sound, no swish of passing traffic, no flushing cisterns or clattering plates. Soon we would see the mistresses as well as the girls. Would Miss

Patrice, Miss Gee's sister, be as strict and stern as her? Tor's bedsprings creaked.

'Are you awake, Tor?'

'I've been awake for ages.'

'Do you think I should plait my hair?'

The neat-fingered one of the family, Tor was good at drawing and making raffia flowers. Her animal drawings were so real you could almost feel them, her writing was tiny but neat. She moved quickly, she learned quickly, she never got in a panic. Though two years younger she was more clever than me. She got out of her bed and huddled under my blankets. Her feet felt cold and small. I rubbed my calves against them while she started combing me. You must remove the tangles before you could make plaits. The hair must be pulled straight and even. It was lovely being close again, almost like our room at home.

'What are you doing, Bonnie? I can hear you. Tor's with you. Can I come too?'

'No, you can't. She's plaiting my hair.'

'Let her,' said Tor.

It was to please Miss Gee that I was suffering this combing and pulling. Tor was patient, she tried not to tweak. She had a kinder nature than I had. In Ireland when the three of us had played grandmother's steps it was Tor who showed Ula what to do. It was Tor who read the names of streets aloud and helped Ula with anything too heavy or tall. Ula was an embarrassment, she walked with her toes turned out, her skirts always looked too long. She was inquisitive and cocksure. At nearly eight she should know how to behave. Tor and I looked like perfect schoolgirls in our uniforms; no one would think we had a runaway mother and a sadly disorganized home.

'You're hurting, Tor. It's pulling me.' My eyes were watering. The hair grew in a fluff on my nape. Tor said you must pull as hard as possible to plait properly. My neck felt stretched and raw.

22

'Your skin looks all red, it's nearly bleeding. Oh stop, Tor, leave her alone.'

Blood and knives terrified Ula, the only things that made her afraid. She had her gas mask in my bed with her, her feet were warm against mine. Tor said she would make one plait like a pony's tail, which wouldn't pull as much. We lay squashed together with our knees tangled. My neck still hurt but my sisters were there. It was easy to make Ula happy, you just had to include her. I wished that Tor spoke more than she did.

Ula said in a kind voice that I was probably nervous this morning because of the other girls.

'I'm not nervous, you fool. But just don't tell anyone about our home.'

'You mean about Mamma leaving us because of Hitler. Don't worry, I won't tell.'

'Not Hitler, stupid. I mean about our home being occupied. Don't talk about Bruno, or Papa ... or anything.'

I meant her friend dying in Ireland. She understood me. She started whispering to her gas mask. Then she tried her whistling.

'Help Tor with my hair, will you? The plait hurts. It's no good.'

Their fingers tickled as they eased the hair out. At last my neck felt normal again. I looked at my face, white and serious, in the mirror over the chest of drawers. Perhaps Mamma would send coloured ribbons to tie in bunches over my ears.

No one had said when we should get up. We pulled the curtains back and got our dressing gowns. I reminded them to say 'dormitory' instead of 'bedroom'. It was 'form' here, not class or schoolroom. We must make the best of it and forget Gov and our old schoolroom. There would be no making raffia flowers here. Tor and I used to play a private game about animals. I was nearly twelve and too

23

old for imaginary games.

Outside a bell rang, the kind of bell pulled by a rope. Did it mean breakfast or should we go to the chapel room? We hurried into our clothes. Ula started being stupid again, wanting to wash her gas mask. Did Miss Gee know what Mamma thought about religion?

'Let's go to the dining room. Food is what I need.' Ula skipped downstairs ahead. The chapel-room door was closed, we could hear voices that seemed to be arguing. One voice sounded tearful. A notice on the door said 'Biblical Tableau Practice 3 pm'.

The dining room was empty. Through the door to the kitchen the old gardener was making breakfast. He wore a sacking apron and thickly soled boots. The boots made him seem taller but he was bent and wizened. He was heating baked beans. There were tinned tomatoes as well.

'Hullo, what's your name? I'm Ula.'

'Oh ah. Gumm.'

He was helping indoors to oblige. He was the gardener by rights. His lock of hair hung over the beans. His moustache made him like a miniature Hitler, he had knotted hands. He smelled like Tor, sweaty, but very strong. Tor had sweated since I could remember. I hoped she wouldn't do it here.

'I like fried bread better than toast, it's what we had in Ireland,' Ula said, squashing her tomatoes till the juice ran pinky brown. She was eating our school colours, red tomatoes and brown fried bread. She offered some to the gas mask. Grease ran down her chin.

Tor wasn't enjoying this food. I moved closer. We had never had baked beans. Her sweating was a worry. She washed a lot. There was no one we could ask. Gov had been too old to know about bodies, Mamma was too busy or away. I asked Gumm for some butter.

'It's margarine, Bonnie, remember it's the war. Where is Miss Gee, please? Is she in the chapel room?'

24

He sniffed. 'She never told me about all this. No staff. No cook. What am I supposed to do? Too much.'

His job was maintaining the property and the grounds. Some people expected too much.

'Do you mean there is no one to run the school now?' Ula leaned forward, licking her fingers.

'Ah, new girls. I trust that you will assist Gumm in any way you can. After today we shall meet in the chapel room and settle our routine.'

She looked as grey and serious as she had yesterday. Had it been her we'd heard crying? She looked critically at my hair. We would adjust to curriculum.

'Who will teach us, Miss Gee? Where is your sister?'

Miss Gee looked at Ula. Miss Patrice would be along presently, she would be our form mistress. Meanwhile we would find text books in our desks. We would use the same form room. There were changes this term, not only on the domestic side, she glanced at Gumm, but academically too. She would announce the changes when the other girls arrived. Meanwhile we should copy the time-table written on the blackboard and pin it inside the lids of our desks. She closed her eyes when she'd finished speaking. Gumm crashed the plates outside.

The form rooms were at the back of the building, with the dormitories above them. They overlooked the croquet lawn and kitchen gardens. More leaves had fallen in the night from the beech tree, scattering the grass in pale brown piles. The form room was a little warmer than the other rooms. The desks, the walls and floor covering were brown. Miss Gee's copperplate handwriting covered the blackboard. Tor read it aloud. There was Biblical Tableau Practice every day. I chose the double desk at the back for Tor and me. We would prop the lid on our heads and talk in private. Ula banged her desk lid in front.

'Tor, shall we be all right here?'

'We'll have to be. There's no choice.'

25

The text books were newer than Gov's ancient ones. We had never owned exercise books before. Tor had her precious diary. Gov had given me a pen and pencil set and Ula some coloured crayons. Gov was as far off as if she were dead. She had taught Tor and me to read and write, we had never been bored with her. I still missed her. Miss Gee had left sheets of brown paper to cover our text books, we must label them with the title and our names.

Tor's thin hands moved precisely. She had finished *Men and Women of History* before my brown paper was creased into shape. There was *Mathematics Made Magic*, the *Geography Lover's Guide* and *Easy French*. The look and feel of the books made me anxious. Tor's writing would be the best in the school. My own was large and childish. We'd never learned tables. Life was best if you did things well. Tor liked learning, Ula tackled anything with gusto but we'd never had to compete. Ula crumpled brown paper in front of us, getting Gripfix in her hair. She was pleased to be doing real work in a real school, with her elder sisters near. She put her rubber in her mouth crossways and started humming.

'You're not a dog with a bone, Ula. Don't hold your pencil like that.'

She went on making dots and scribbles, pressing dents into the paper. How the girls would jeer.

'What, Ula, are you doing, pray?'

'Hullo Miss Gee, I'm just busy with something. I am looking forward to sums.'

'Bona, you as the eldest should have shown your little sister what to do. Look at this book. I am disappointed.'

'I'm sorry, Miss Gee. You see Ula can't quite read yet. She could never manage *Tiny Tales of Yore*. I'll cover it for her when I've finished mine.'

'Not read? What a disgrace.'

'Mamma didn't agree with a lot of lessons. I'm Bonnie, you know, not Bona.'

'I prefer the full nomenclature. No lessons at all, you say? What a tragedy. What negligence.'

'What's negligence?' Ula was jaunty. Tor read her anything that she needed to know. As long as she had us nothing upset her. Miss Gee said it was assumed that her girls could read and write prior to arrival here.

'But we aren't really your girls, are we, Miss Gee? We belong to our Mamma.'

'Shut up, Ula.'

Miss Gee said that I should allow Ula to express herself. Self-expression, self-governance, self-determination were admirable. Magnolia House aimed at democracy. She added that Ula was entrusted to her care, in one sense she did belong to Miss Gee.

I hated to think that this might be true. It was war, there was no one else, we must obey her. The lessons, especially that biblical one, sounded ridiculous. I dreaded the arrival of the girls. I smiled.

'It's quite absurd I know. But Ula *is* backward. What *shall* we do with her?'

'We are not equipped for retarded pupils. Learning should start early and end late. I emphasize the need for prolonged application for all three of you. Hortense, that handwriting is far too cramped. As well as lessons we aim at elegance, that inner grace, some call it "*je ne sais quoi*".'

We looked blank. She wrote our names on separate sheets of paper. When the book binding was completed we should practise writing copperplate, repeating our names until we reached the foot of the page. Ula must hold her pencil correctly, in the right hand please, and do not press. I liked my writing, Tor's print was beautiful. It was insulting to be told to change.

'Slowly Ula, do not touch the line above or the line beneath.'

'I like it large,' Ula said, pressing and breathing aloud. With her rubber back in her mouth she was happy. Miss

Gee walked between the desks. She paused at the black-board. She erased 'gymnastics', substituting another lesson of Biblical Tableau practice.

'What is that, Miss Gee, please?'

She said it was the important subject this term in particular. The school enacted a pageant every Christmas which parents came to watch; it was the yearly tradition. She took Ula's gas mask, she showed us the hooks on the wall. All masks must be hung there during lessons. As government property they must be treated with respect.

'And perhaps, Bona, you will be good enough to refill the ink-wells. Ink replenishment is a monitor's task.'

'Does it mean I'll be a monitor?'

Prefects and monitors were elected yearly by the two head girls, at present Phoebe Pillcock and Margaret Pierce.

The heavy stone bottle slipped in my hand. Miss Gee had left the room. Ula said the ink smelled like Gumm's apron, cross and bitter. Don't sniff at it, it could be poisonous. She was longing to write in ink. With her steady hand she was as diligent as Tor. By the time she reached the bottom of her page her name was neat. I filled each ink-well with care. If I was made a monitor I would see that my sisters were well treated.

Ula hoped that Miss Gee's sister would be as nice as she was. I despaired of Ula. Couldn't she understand that Miss Gee was an enemy? We should distrust her until we knew her better. We should tread warily and try to please.

We waited in the conservatory behind the magnolia. No one could see us; we could watch the girls arrive. There were no plants there except for one dying cheeseplant. We could see the unicorn again, wise and aloof in the daylight.

One by one the taxis and cars drove through the gate, pulling up in front of our tree. Seen from this side its branches were like a face, the criss-cross boughs making wrinkles.

Except for one girl they came with their parents, who came into the school with their daughters in the proper expected manner. Some of the fathers were in uniform. Though serving they had found time to come and talk to Miss Gee, to leave instructions regarding their girls. Voices murmured from behind the study door about extra French, piano practice and games. Miss Gee's door opened and closed.

The parents looked sad-eyed when they left. Mothers and daughters cried and clung, fathers cleared their throats. We had a good view of these partings shielded by our magnolia. We watched the final waving, the wiping of forlorn tears. It started to rain. The unicorn looked on with blank eyes.

'Now it's a proper school full of proper girls.' Ula hopped round the cheeseplant. We could hear the girls in the hall. Minutes earlier their faces had been wet with tears. They recovered quickly. They shouted catch phrases. 'Don't be so *feeble*', 'Same to you with double knobs on', 'I admire you more than somewhat', 'Oh catch me someone, ere I swoon'. The laughter sounded false, so soon after the farewells. Timidly we left the conservatory.

With faces pink and dry again the girls shook the rain from their hair. The aura of parents' fur coats, morocco leather and cigars was replaced by costly shampoo, well-scrubbed skin and laundered clothes. No one noticed us, they were engrossed in their reunion.

So we went back to the form room again to practise more writing. At our desk at the back of the room was the tall girl I had seen earlier who had come without parents or friends. I had noticed her pale hair, the way it hung round her cheeks and neck. She was looking at my pen and pencil set.

'Three sisters. My oh my.'

# THREE

Phoebe was my first meeting with a real live schoolgirl. I would never forget her name or her face. She spoke slowly, drawlingly, her movements seeming slower because of her height. Her skin reminded me of moonstones, a kind of transparency. She had long-fingered hands. Her faintly greasy hair was pushed behind her ears. Her eyes seemed colourless, staring unblinkingly.

'I can tell you've been here for ages. Your uniform is so old.'

'Don't be so cheeky, Ula.'

'Your infant sister is right. It's more than ages. It feels as if I came before the flood.'

Her skirt was skimpy, with worn seams, her jersey sleeves were too short. The jersey was back to front, the vee neck backwards; her sleeves were pushed up to give a short-sleeved effect.

I had felt so proud of my uniform. I felt fussy now, overdressed. I wanted my own hair in a low parting with a pushed-back fringe, to wear my own clothes back to front. She crossed her arms, gripping the elbows, she spoke with her long chin raised. She preferred rags to a new uniform. She was just living for the day when she left this prison; she'd be sixteen soon, praise be.

'I like this school, Phoebe. This is my writing. Miss Gee told us that you were the head girl.'

I said quickly that Ula was slow at writing, but she didn't glance at Ula's page. She asked if we had any brothers.

'No, we haven't.' I spoke quickly before Ula could start talking about Bruno. I said my age and that I wasn't sure yet about school.

'I have one brother. A godsend, *je vous assure*.'

'Why "godsend", Phoebe? What is "*je vous* ..."'? We did have ...'

'Ula talks too much, she's impossible.'

Phoebe smiled without interest. She said that we were only allowed outside the school with a relative. The Gee sisters had a complex about safety. Her brother collected her whenever possible. There was a hotel in the town, the Black Lion, did we know it? They served decent cocktails there.

'We saw you arrive in a taxi. Are your parents away as well?'

They were dead, she said, but not unhappily; she didn't feel the loss. Her uncle in America was her guardian. Sometimes she spent her holidays there. Once or twice she had stayed here, at school. Her closest friend and relative was her brother. She and Midge organized the school.

'Midge? Is that Margaret?'

'No one says "Margaret". Take no notice of what Miss Gee says. She's too old to be running a school. Her ideas are antique.'

Perhaps Phoebe would be here in the coming holidays. I would learn to move and smile like her. And she was clever, speaking French and travelling by taxi alone.

'Where is the younger Miss Gee? We haven't met her.'

'Probably still trying to locate some staff. Not that it

makes a difference. The teaching here barely exists.'

She went to the blackboard, rubbed out Biblical Tableau practice and substituted gym. She yawned. Her teeth were square and big. She had a large pointed tongue.

'Come on, everyone, let's go and unpack our things.'

Her red leather luggage had been taken up, her suitcase had labels of hotels in foreign countries. She loved and was used to travel. She piled quantities of clothes on her bed. Not much longer for her in this feeble and antique place, praise be.

'That isn't uniform, Phoebe. What are those clothes?'

Ula picked up a green frock with smocking across the yoke. Phoebe took it back and held it to her chest. A frock like green woollen cobweb, a frock for a grown-up.

'Mufti, of course. I'm not staying in these rags all day.'

'Mufti? What's that?'

I guessed it would be something to discourage us. It seemed that everyone wore their own home clothes at night except for the little ones. We were the new girls; we would look different, every night.

Phoebe went on throwing clothes about, she had no idea of my dismay. Tor wasn't the same, clothes didn't affect her or Ula so much. Another dress of holly-berry red, more sweaters in beautiful shades, a velvet bolero to match a skirt. I looked at Tor; she ought to realize, our uniforms were not enough. Each night we would stand out like fun figures. Would all their clothes be like Phoebe's, luxurious and distinct? She went on casually handling the soft shantungs and linens. She had a jewellery box with seed pearls in it and a string of coral beads. Why hadn't Mamma read the prospectus properly? Phoebe was putting on high-heeled velvet shoes.

'Oh Phoebe, wear the green dress to match the shoes, they're lovely.'

Ula was like a jester, jumping about, waiting on Phoebe the queen. She didn't envy Phoebe, she just liked serving her. Phoebe changed casually without drawing her curtains, standing white and tall in her vest.

'You've got lollopers, Phoebe, I can see them. Bonnie's aren't as big.'

'Be quiet, Ula. Shut up, can't you?'

'Don't be severe on the infant, she's harmless. The girls here call them *"pommes"*.'

There was a lot of school jargon to learn it seemed, mostly words to do with bodily growth. I felt hot and uneasy, I didn't want to know about it. Often I just wished to stay a child. I wanted a figure like Phoebe's without the pain of growing, the pain of change. The higher you were in the school, the more jargon, to be kept a secret from the rest. Phoebe puffed herself proudly under the green smocking. She had brassières if she wanted, too. She settled the soft pleats over her thighs. She didn't want to know about us or what we were feeling, she was interested in herself.

'Can I brush your hair, Phoebe?' Ula waved her tortoiseshell-backed brush. Phoebe had her hair cut expensively in London, and singed to get rid of split ends. She showed us, she smoothed her parting. She wanted no infants banging her head with a brush. At Christmas her brother would take her to nightclubs, she'd wear a backless gown and spindly golden heels. That was providing her brother was still in the country. He'd joined the army. Lucky beast.

'Why lucky? Will the war last long, do you think?'

She hoped it would last long enough for her to join up. She admired her reflection, she clicked her heels and gave a salute. How much pocket money had we brought with us?

'What pocket money, Phoebe?'

The horror was starting again. Couldn't our family get anything right about coming to school?

'You mean you didn't realize? *Zut alors!* No money at all

34

to buy anything? You'll need some. The food here is muck.'

Each girl brought money, Miss Gee encouraged it. Miss Patrice kept a Saturday shop. You could buy stamps, soap and stationery. There was jam, fruit, biscuits, even eggs. Phoebe said I should write home and ask for money. Was our father serving in the forces?

'Oh he died. Ages ago, like your father.' I spoke quickly before Ula started again about death and disaster. But Phoebe was only interested in her own family. Her parents had died in an Indian earthquake. She had her rich uncle and her brother. No complaints. Brothers had friends, especially in the army, brothers could be useful. Was she thinking of boyfriends?

'Our mother is in the army, in a way she is.'

'The ATS? Why didn't you say?'

'She's going to entertain troops, as a singer. She was going to go into films.'

'A film star? You've succeeded in impressing me. I'm all ears. Tell me more.'

It wasn't true. There was nothing to tell her unless I invented it. Mamma had spoken about film work before the war. I knew nothing about films, I'd never seen one. I'd never been to a play. Ula used to cut pictures from film magazines with our cook in the kitchen. I didn't know a single film star's name. Phoebe's interest waned, I might have known it would. She went on admiring her hair, smiling to herself. If I'd answered she wouldn't have heard.

There were noises outside. 'Here they are, here comes everyone. Midge, I've been longing for you more than somewhat. You're here at last.'

Footsteps, voices, laughter, our future schoolmates crowded in. Cases banged, curtains rattled, hats and coats hurled through the air. Gasping, grimacing, shrieking, shoving. 'Same to you with double knobs on', 'Catch me

35

someone ere I swoon'.

'Midge. At last.'

She was another tall girl with little dark eyes and bright cheeks. When she laughed her eyes creased into their sockets. She had very curly hair. All the faces looked pretty and confident, all smiling, all with friends. These were our future companions, squabbling over beds and cases, swapping holiday experiences, not asking us our names. 'My dear it was *him*, he actually *smiled* at me.' 'We were going on this cruise but Daddy wouldn't, he cancelled it. The *political* situation, my dear.' 'Has Gubgub lost weight? Hold me ere I swoon again.'

Gubgub was the plump one with red hair and a bangle above one elbow that looked too tight to be pulled down. Did all schoolgirls look and talk like this? Were they all affected and boastful, waving their brassières around?

A tiny girl with a face like a monkey said that the waiter had stared at her pommes. 'Every time. Can you imagine?'

'My dear Barbie, have you any pommes? I hadn't noticed.'

'You're cruel, Phoebe. How is your brother? And how is you-know-who?'

'Hush, mice have ears.'

Phoebe was the most exciting, Gubgub was the fattest and the most giggling, fingering her gold bangle. Barbie was the one they teased. I liked Midge's face, she seemed the friendliest. Phoebe said tonight she would sleep near the film star's daughters. Tomorrow she might move away. Midge and she were a team, friends of long standing, they sat close on her bed, whispering. Midge had delicate thin ankles, the rubber soles of her shoes were newly heeled. I had spilled ink on my blouse sleeve, I rubbed at it. I would wear my jersey turned back to front and push the sleeves up. I would stick out my chest and pull my cheeks in to look alluring. I parted my hair differently, combing it flat. Midge smiled at me.

'You haven't said your name yet. I'm Midge.'

'I know. A midge is a mosquito.'

She didn't mind me saying it, she smiled with her eyes. I felt I could trust her. I said our names and that I was worried about pocket money, stamps and mufti clothes. Her eyes seemed like gleaming slits of kindness. She had lots of stamps and clothes didn't matter. She had no interest in clothes or high heels. Which did I prefer, gym or games?

'We never did either. This is our first school. I'm dreading French and maths.'

She understood about liking to kick dead leaves or run on damp grass. She said I shouldn't worry about Biblical Tableau practice, it was just one of Miss Gee's fads. She treated me as an equal, not a newcomer. She had a large family of brothers and sisters. She was the eldest. She loved and missed her home. When she'd first come here she'd suffered from homesickness; she liked to welcome new girls now. I told her about our house being empty and how the army would be moving in. About my sisters and me being backward about lessons, about Ula letting us down. I knew that when there was privacy I would tell her about Ula's dark secret, how a child had died at her hand. And also how Bruno had died of croup after Tor and I had undressed him and left him naked under the Christmas tree. She was trustworthy and understanding.

'Sit by me at supper,' she said. I was chosen. I raised my chin to show my smooth neck rising from my jersey.

On the first night the girls ate alone without any staff present. No staff had been seen this term. We heard the crashing of plates in the kitchen, the squeaking of trolley wheels. The little girls treated Gumm with cheekiness, unafraid of his Hitler frown. 'Gumm, Gumm, eat your chewing gum.' Ula joined in excitedly.

It was cold corned beef and the potatoes were hard. Some of the girls had supplies of dried fruit and biscuits.

37

Their voices shrieked above the plates and cutlery noises. 'Golly gumdrops, this meat is antique.' 'Catch me ere I swoon.'

Midge was by me, Tor on my other side, Ula was opposite, gobbling everything she could. Tor ate a little meat. The smell of the dining room took away my appetite. Midge, Phoebe and Gubgub were an accepted threesome. There were three little girls as young as Ula. The tiny girl with the face of a monkey was like a midget with Shirley Temple hair. She was thirteen.

Phoebe languished over her plate; she yawned hugely. 'I can't eat this. Give it to the hungry new girl.'

They all laughed and looked at Ula. I hated them but Ula didn't care, eating the food with enjoyment.

'Take no notice,' Tor whispered. 'Don't let them see you mind.'

Phoebe ate a banana that she'd brought with her. She licked it, her long jaw moving slowly, her long fingers barely touching the fruit. Except for Midge and the little ones they'd all changed for supper. Dresses vied with pinafore-topped skirts and thin blouses. Each girl had a cherished look. They picked at Gumm's supper and chattered.

'Enough, enough,' Phoebe called, flapping the banana skin on the table edge. 'I can't hear myself think. Remember the film star's daughters are here.'

I went red. Ula piped, 'She's not a film star. Mamma is singing for soldiers.'

'*Mamma*?' There was a chorus of mirth. '*Mamma*? You did say Mamma? Oh catch me Mamma ere I swoon.'

'Where did you spring from, Mamma's daughters? Did you come from Mars? How too antique for words.'

Ula laughed with them, she didn't understand malice. Tor and I looked at our plates.

'She's their mother whatever they call her or whatever she does. Leave them alone, they're new.'

38

I might have known Midge would stick up for us. Phoebe got up and left the dining room. Come on everyone, time for the game. The rest followed her in a flock.

'What is this game, Midge, please?'

It was played on the first night of each term. It was called 'Raiding', the whole school played. You picked sides. You took turns travelling from one end of the dormitory to the other by swinging on the curtain rails. If you touched the ground you were out. The trick was to lift yourself high, using your shoulders, swinging your hips and knees. You undressed and got into pyjamas first.

The basins thumped back and forth, plugs gurgled, lights flashed on and off. No one cared to remember black-out curtains or saving hot water, 'Raiding' mattered more than war. Ula brushed her teeth excitedly. She would play a real game at last. Tor was sweating, she was nervous. She hated being despised or mocked.

'The little ones can stay with me, Phoebe. You and Gub-gub head the teams.'

Midge guessed that Tor was frightened; no one need play if they didn't want to. 'Raiding' needed courage and strong arms. Tor kept her company on the bed with the little ones. I wouldn't show fear, I would try. I must make Midge and Phoebe admire me, my sisters would be proud of me.

'I'll have the film star's daughter. You, Bonnie, come with me.' Phoebe had picked me, I'd been elected. I would be gossamer light, quick as a bird. I would reach the basins without a falter, they would see I wasn't antique or quaint. Tor was on the bed with Ula, wringing her fingers. Ula had wanted to play but hadn't complained. Her white lock of hair was my mascot, their sympathy gave me strength.

The beds were pushed apart, the curtains drawn back tightly. My turn now, the railings are cold. My clean hands slip on the iron, I'm moving. One hand over the

39

other, watch me swing. I'm flying like an angel, watch me, Ula. Look, Midge, I can do it. Lift your hips, swing your knees, work your shoulders, don't look down. Watch the curtain rail, watch your fingers, my sisters are cheering, they believe in me. 'Come on, Bonnie. Bonn-ee.' Little Barbie is weightless. Gubgub has fallen. Watch your hands, don't look down. My arms ache, my chest hurts, I'll show them. We're Mamma's children, you owe her respect. She's better than a film star, she's perfect. 'Bonn-ee. Bonn-ee.' She left us without pocket money or mufti, she's perfect, she's our mamma. Barbie, the midget, is wearing a nightdress, her toes are like sparrow's claws. Phoebe's pyjamas are piped creamy satin, whatever she does or has she's the best. Watch me, I'm a flying angel. Look Ula, look Midge, look Tor.

'Ah. Aaah. What a shame.'

I heard the groan before I realized I'd fallen. I had banged my foot, lost my grip. The curtains broke the fall, I slithered and flopped, my heels hit the floor, Barbie fell after me. There's only Phoebe. Phoebe won, she always does.

'Not bad, Bonnie, considering you're a novice. For a first attempt not bad.'

Someone laughed. I sat by Tor. She knew I felt vanquished. I was panting, I wasn't beaten. I would teach them to laugh.

'I say, can anyone here do the splits? Watch, this is how you do it.'

I had never tried any acrobatics, another voice had come from my mouth. You stretched one foot forward firmly, the other one behind, you went down. You could do anything if you made up your mind to it. It is will-power and determination. Push down, never mind the pain.

Phoebe watched and smiled. She put a foot before her, she sank like a bird on wings. Her thin legs settled at right angles to her body, she put her hands above her head, she watched me, she smiled at me.

'Phoebe, you're wonderful, you're the tops. I admire you more than somewhat.'

They cheer her, they congratulate her because they love her. Darling Phoebe is sublime.

I have pain in my thighs and humiliation. I have been punished for showing off. No one can outdo Phoebe the wonderful; I feel so ashamed I could die. I cannot die, my sisters need me. I must keep the promise to Mamma. It's Tor I worry most about, she's so thin and silent, she's not spoken to anyone here. This school is too grand, these girls are different, they are rich, we'll never fit in. They are cruel, they're contemptuous and shallow. Trying the splits has given me a pain.

In the night I woke up with the pain again. I walked barefooted between the beds, each containing a sleeping girl curled into various shaped lumps. The lavatory light was on. I must not pity myself, mustn't cry. It's just a pain, I'm not frightened. If a bomb came down I wouldn't care now, if my sisters died with me. Blood in my pyjamas, it can't be. Don't scream, it might be a dream. I will wake up in bed having dreamed of an air raid. A rusty splotch of red in my dream. I have injured myself inside from showing off, I tried the splits, now I'm paid. It's a dream of an air raid, a dream of a game, don't be frightened.

I leaned over my knees, I heard myself cry. Midge came to my help again. She pushed the lavatory door. Come, Bonnie, you're not dying, stop that crying. You're just menstruating, someone should have told you. About that blood coming, running and red. Blood that would come every month, nothing to do with splits, just menstruation. You would have it for most of your life.

'Don't men have it? It's disgusting.'

'Men don't have anything. It's to do with having a child. It hurts sometimes, it's nothing serious, even if you do have pains.'

She hadn't started yet, but she was ready for it. She had sanitary pads in her drawer. The older girls brought them in preparation. Sometimes they called it 'the flag'. The little ones didn't know about it. The older ones had their own lavatory. I might as well get used to the idea and be practical. It was how women were made.

I began to feel less afraid and more curious. I had learned an important secret of the school. I was a woman now, Midge told me, not like Tor and Ula. I'd never be quite the same, never be young again.

When I was in bed I thought Phoebe whispered something.

'Well, well, put out the flags.'

I got up early to look again. The pad had smudgy marks like the writing of a thick nibbed pen.

# FOUR

Having no pocket money or mufti was bad. Not knowing
what to say was worse. We had never mixed with anyone,
let alone children. There was the worry of the school
slang. I must make Phoebe like me, I hoped that Midge
already did. Showing off was frowned on. I heard Gubgub
say that I was a swank. The thought that I would be a
woman once a month was comforting. I mustn't mess my
new pyjamas. Being a woman could be a messy nuisance
in spite of the importance you gained. Midge didn't mind
being a late starter, you might go on having that blood for
at least thirty years. If you had a baby it would stop for a
while. Midge was shocked over my ignorance. Babies,
bodies, growing and blood were both lovely and awful, it
was best to realize and understand as soon as you could.
Being frightened was a hindrance. Knowing things early
was best.

Gov must have considered these things too secret to be
mentioned. We had never asked questions about our
bodies, we stuck to knitting and raffia flowers. Midge gave
me another towel rather reluctantly. Don't use it unless
absolutely necessary, she said. She had a secret use for her
towels that no one knew about. She might show me when

the right moment came. I wanted to please her, but I didn't know how to stop the blood coming. I would try and let it drip into the lavatory if I could. At her home, she said, her family were open about everything; it made a difference to life.

'What is this secret, Midge?'

She would show me on Sunday if she could. I was to write to my mother and ask for the biggest pads. 'Remember, Bonnie, the largest, that's all I'm saying now.'

There were three sizes. The outsize ones were called Maternity wear. The one I was wearing felt like a rabbit's tail. I needn't have worried, though, the blood stopped coming the next day. As I grew older my cycle would settle, Midge told me. Don't forget the letter to my mother.

School assembled in the chapel room. I looked forward to seeing Miss Patrice. The sisters didn't always agree, it seemed. Miss Patrice believed in more practical and physical pastimes. There were other ways of achieving inner elegance and grace besides Bible studies and handwriting. She would have been happy to teach tree felling or dairy farming; as it was she taught us games.

Miss Gee stood on the dais in the chapel room, still wearing grey with a white blouse. Miss Patrice was by her. She was quite different, with a big face and mottled, sallow skin. Her long lashes looked out of place, her eyes were brown and large as a cow's. She watched but she didn't join in the hymns and prayers required by her sister. Ula liked singing, she liked showing that she knew the tune though she couldn't read the words. 'There's no discouragement, Shall make him once relent, His first avowed intent to be a pilgrim.' I could see that Miss Patrice didn't agree with religion. Midge said that Miss Gee was high church. I imagined a tall steeple and a choir that sang very high notes. Miss Gee gave thanks for the school comradeship and good food. We prayed to win the war and our soul's guidance, we prayed to retain pure hearts. I moved my lips, I wanted to fit in, I thought of Mamma again. I didn't think it was true that she'd miss us. I missed and thought about her still. She ought to know that I was beginning to become a woman. This praying was the final straw.

Midge had showed me the prefects' lavatory near the boiler room. In the corner was an enamel bin for used pads. The stained lumps wrapped in paper gave a sweetish rotten smell when you lifted the lid. It was called the 'flag bin' by the prefects.

'But I'm not a prefect, Midge. Are you sure?'

'I'm sure I'm sure. You'll be a prefect. Phoebe and I choose.'

I felt too new to be a prefect. I was wrongly dressed, without pocket money or knowledge of French. Under the cover of singing, Phoebe hissed, 'How is Mamma's girl this morning? Put out the flag yet?' She turned her blind-looking eyes to the window before I could tell her I was a prefect. She had combed her hair so flat you could see her scalp through it; she was still beautiful, though she had as much colour as a piece of string.

The praying and singing ended. Miss Patrice took her place on the dais. She had an announcement to make which was more in the nature of a request. The present emergency was testing; we must memorize the national slogans. 'Dig for Victory', 'Save for the Brave', 'Careless Talk Costs Lives'. My sisters and I knew no one in the forces, whose whereabouts we might let slip to the enemy, though we'd liked to see them passing in lorries. Soon soldiers would sleep in our home. Phoebe's brother was going to be an officer, Gubgub had a cousin at sea. Various girls' fathers had positions in the Admiralty or the War Office, where they would probably stay until peace was declared. Miss Patrice spoke of saving soap, and the economical use of stationery. We could save on laundry by

45

taking extra care with our clothes. Meanwhile her Saturday shop opened each week, the proceeds of which went towards the war. Now for her special announcement regarding digging for victory. Each of us was to own a garden plot and grow vegetables. We would plant and eat our own potatoes with pride.

Midge put her hand up. 'Does it mean we should take orders from Gumm?'

'Midge, you have anticipated me.' She spoke about the reduction in numbers of pupils and of staff. At the present time there was just Miss Gee and herself. The girls looked glad. It seemed that the two sisters were to teach all lessons this term. For the sake of convenience we would work in one form. She relied on her prefects and monitors to help the younger girls in need of coaching. Her eyes were a warm fudgy brown, she spoke with missionary zeal. How could I coach anyone when I knew nothing? I was used to Tor helping me. Gumm was to take over all the cooking.

'What about games?' Midge asked.

Miss Patrice looked strained. It was a question of the croquet lawn and the front lawn; which was to be used for games and which for the allotments? Miss Gee tapped her ruler on the edge of her hymn book. The front lawn must remain untouched. No ball games, running feet or digging spades must sully the grass in front. The green peace of the school entrance must remain undisturbed. No digging or ball games in front.

So the croquet lawn must be sacrificed for the growing of home produce. The chapel room must be sacrificed for the use of indoor games. Was this why the sisters had been arguing yesterday morning? Miss Gee's chapel room was also the strongest room in the building. Until a shelter could be built, it would be used during air raids as a place of safety.

'So, girls,' Miss Patrice called decisively. 'Indoor games

indoors. The croquet lawn to be dug into plots.'

'And girls,' reminded Miss Gee, 'remember your gas masks, carry them at all times, make use of the gas mask hooks.'

Midge explained the Off Games book. Those who had the flag could sign their names there. The sisters didn't agree over this either. Miss Gee allowed you to lie on your bed and feel delicate. Miss Patrice was brisk; it was self-indulgent to give in, a run with a skipping rope round the lawn was her remedy. Differences over religion, menstruation and the use of the grounds were causes of friction. Barbie, the tiny girl, liked to eavesdrop, she had heard them argue in their private quarters beyond the conservatory. The sisters vied for power. Gubgub had once woken to find Miss Gee bending over her with a hot-water bottle. They referred to the flag as 'the time of the month' or 'being off colour'.

The chapel room had no equipment for use as a gymnasium, no parallel bars, no springboards, mats or ropes.

I signed my name in the book with the pencil attached by a rubber band; I wrote in copperplate. I was pleased not to have to leap with a skipping rope and run the risk of spoiling Midge's clean pad.

'Don't look so glum,' Miss Patrice said. She had a bouncing walk, moving on the balls of her feet. The creases of her pleated tunic scarcely moved, remaining sharp. You couldn't imagine her in anything but a dark blouse and navy serge but she must have once been young. Had those fudge-coloured eyes ever loved? The younger girls became giggly when she came near. 'Catch me, hold me someone, it's *her*.' But they didn't mean it, they were showing off. Midge said that both sisters were too old for their job, that the present poor staffing was their own fault, nothing to do with the war. They misman-aged, staff didn't want to stay here. The school was badly planned, badly managed without enough space for games. The rush of new entries that they'd hoped for turned out to be just me and my sisters. The girls left this school with few educational attainments. Some went on to finishing schools. Phoebe's uncle had planned to send her to Switzerland. Because of the war she hoped it would be the ATS instead.

Miss Patrice told me to walk round the croquet lawn while the others did indoor games. While they jumped their ropes or passed clubs from hand to hand I would kick leaves outside again in my boots. I heard them shouting. Was that Ula laughing? There was the hoop she had pushed her foot into, there was the mound of dead leaves and the molehill. I was alone and it was autumn. I was still happy with the Wellingtons.

The school pageant was planned for 21 December. There was Biblical Tableau practice every day. Miss Gee tapped a rhythm on the radiator with her ruler while the girls walked round the dais. The little ones sang in the corner. Bedspreads were wrapped round the older ones to make them appear biblical; they were portraying ancient times. Midge was Moses, holding the stone tablets up. I didn't know the difference between the Old and New Testament. I knew about the birth of Jesus but not much else. I dreaded being asked to sing. 'I'm off games, Miss Gee.' Perhaps she would let me lie down.

'Join the little ones in the corner and sing.' It was the same hymn.

'Sing up, Bona, I cannot hear.'

'Though fancies flee away, I'll fear not what men say, I'll labour . . .'

'Enough, Bona. Stop singing. You are tone deaf. I suspected it from your speaking voice. Just move your lips to the words.'

I blushed deeply. Everyone had heard. The film star's daughter couldn't sing a note, she had an ugly speaking voice. How more than somewhat bad.

Miss Gee leaned closer towards Ula's singing face. Ula knew she sang well. Miss Gee smiled with radiance.

'A natural soprano, pure and high. Sing, Ula, as loud as you can. Bona, you had better go and help with the bedspreads. Then sit down and keep quiet.'

'Well well, wardrobe maid,' Phoebe said, in contempt of the whole affair. Religion, gym and pageants were nonsense to be endured until she joined the army. I pictured her relaxing in officers' bars with a peaked cap on her head. Long cigarettes would dangle from her pale fingers while the officers declared their love.

I couldn't help feeling proud and delighted with Ula, though I was jealous too. As the leading choir girl she would wear angel's wings and sing a solo. I supposed I would have to settle bedspreads to fall round her toes and comb her hair fluffily. Our Irish cook must have taught her to sing. We would have no one to come and watch the pageant. I would beg Mamma to come. I hadn't written yet, because of the embarrassment of asking for sanitary towels.

'Dear Mamma. Please will you try and come to our play at Christmas? Also could you send some stamps? The other girls change each night into other clothes but we can't. Love from Bonnie.'

On Sunday I saw Midge's secret. In a way it altered my life. She led the way past the croquet lawn, down the path to the potting sheds. At the end of the garden was Gumm's hut with a corrugated tin roof and a large metal incinerator on legs with an odd chimney-like lid.

'Where's the surprise? What is that awful smell?'

'It's for burning rubbish. It smells worse when it's just been lit.'

It was Gumm's job to see to the incinerator. The surprise was in his hut. We were out of bounds, but there was no one to see us. We pushed open the door of his hut.

Midge said that in summertime he sat with his pipe and a flask of tea. The war had changed his life too; now he was indoors cooking meals. There were bundles of newspapers and sticks there. Under some sacking in the corner was the surprise.

'Midge. I had no idea. Can I hold it?'

'Not yet. She must get to know you.'

She had trusted me with her secret pet. I felt suddenly different. My face felt as if it had broken. I hadn't smiled for so long, not since Ireland. I knew Midge's secret and the whole world had improved.

We watched her run to the bars expectantly, sniffing and tame. When she smelled Midge's fingers her whiskers trembled, her nose and forepaws raised. She ran to the exercise wheel, paddling her paws on it; the wheel squeaked as it turned. Then she came back to Midge's fingers. Was she hungry?

'How do you know it's a she mouse?'

'It's obvious, can't you see? That's why we need sanitary pads, her babies should be born soon.'

Midge had a pad in her raincoat pocket. I helped to undo the gauze. We tore the wool into fluff, we relined the nesting box at the other end of the cage. Cleanliness was important, she told me, the nest must be warm and fresh. Mice were nervous, they took fright easily, if threatened they might kill their young. We fed her with toast fragments, we fetched fresh water from the tap outside. An apple core or a carrot was good for them but their basic diet was oats. Milk was good for nursing mothers but too much made their urine smell. The cage had an enchanting frowstiness. I pressed my face closer. Midge had trusted me, I trusted her, I didn't feel anxious or alone. I asked timidly about the babies. How did they get out, how did they start? I added that I did know about it of course, but I'd forgotten. The details had slipped my mind. Would she remind me? I knew she would not hold me in scorn.

She explained patiently about the mouse's life cycle, from birth and copulation to death. She showed me the enlarged stomach, the little entrance under the tail. It happened there, the male mouse put in the seeds, eighteen to twenty days later the babies came out. She kissed the sweet nose lovingly. Nature was magic, wasn't it? Those dots were nipples for breast feeding. She ate a lot, especially now. Getting to the hut was a difficulty sometimes, that was why Midge had made herself a garden prefect. I would be her garden assistant now. I would have the authority to keep the others away. She spoke of pets in general while the mouse's nose went on quivering.

At Midge's home each child owned something, a rat, rabbit, guinea pig or bird. That was how she knew about animals. The pets were allowed in the house at Christmas to run freely beneath the tree. The family sang carols and opened presents while the animals looked on. We'd never had presents or a tree like other people. The one that Tor and I had when we'd undressed Bruno had been a stunted little lopsided larch, not a proper tree. It was the night following that he'd caught his croup and died. No one had said it was our fault, but they thought it. Like Ula's knifing episode in Ireland, it wasn't mentioned. Midge's Christmas sounded lovely, with other children, presents and singing, candles and exciting food. This year I would be here with just my sisters.

'I'll give you one of the babies if you like, Bonnie.'

'Midge. Are you sure?'

'I'm sure I'm sure. But absolutely no one must know. No one at all.'

'I swear it. You can trust me.'

'Not even Phoebe knows about the mouse. Don't ever let me down.'

'She's your best friend, isn't she? She's not like you.'

'We've known each other for years. I understand Phoebe. She's not as confident as you might think. She

51

needs to impress everyone, sometimes it makes her cruel.'

Then I told Midge about our family secrets. About Ula killing her friend. About our brother dying after being left naked to catch cold. How we never mentioned these sad awful happenings. She swore that she'd never tell. But said that some secrets were less frightening if other people knew them, someone who understood and didn't lay blame. I felt relieved to have told her. I would have trusted her with my life.

'When can I have the mouse?'

I must be patient, she said, they weren't even born yet. And mind, Bonnie, not a soul must know. No pets were allowed in this school, the Gees didn't approve. They believed that their girls should show kindness to each other rather than to pets. Their policy of self-governance was muddled when it came to animals and religion.

At supper Phoebe waved a letter from her brother. He'd started his officers' course. Then he might take off for anywhere. How she envied him. Join the army and see life.

# FIVE

I waited for an answer from Mamma. She didn't write but a parcel arrived.

'Look Tor. Oh Tor. Look.'

Mamma had gone to Liberty's again. Now we too could wear angora wool at supper time, we too had patent leather shoes. The dresses had wide collars and belts that laced in front with a thong instead of buckling. Oh look. We're as good as Phoebe now. And I knew something about Midge that Phoebe didn't know. Midge and I trusted each other. I had felt the mouse tail curving my wrist, felt the cool prick of its claws. Mamma had no time to write, she had too much on her mind. She had found time to go to London for our sakes, she had remembered our sizes in clothes. She had remembered that I liked blue. Blue stood for hope and remembrance, blue for the colour of our eyes. Had she paused at the perfume counter on her return? I sniffed the dress, was that her scent? Had she sipped tea and nibbled a sandwich at the same restaurant, while the band played that dreaming tune? Lovely colour, lovely material, lovely unpressed pleats. Who cared about stamps, pocket money or sanitary pads. Before long I would own a mouse. The mother mustn't be disturbed for three weeks after the birth, when the babies would grow fur and open their eyes. You must separate the males from the females before they started interbreeding. I felt clever and knowing now about mice. I put my blue frock on, I felt like dancing. Something rustled, something in the pocket, something more, another surprise.

'Look Tor, another present.'

Mamma had bought me a precious keepsake because I was the oldest, I was the one in charge. The hands were shaped like little arrows on the gold face. It had a rapid tick. It was valuable, it was nicer than Phoebe's. I would put it under my pillow at night. Midge had a cheap one, her parents were not well off. Her brothers and sisters went to grammar schools and lived at home. She and Phoebe had come here at the same time, which must be why they were friends. We all slept in one dormitory now and worked in one class. When the Gee sisters left us alone we did as we liked. Midge, Gubgub and Phoebe helped with the younger ones. No one mentioned French or maths. The form room was warm when we were all in it. Only the gas mask hooks on the wall were a reminder of war.

The croquet lawn was disappearing to be replaced by plots. First the croquet hoops were taken up, the grass dug over. The rabbits and moles must find new homes. Tor and I shared a plot, Ula was next to us. Our fingernails broke, our backs ached but we were close. I longed to confide my plans for mouse ownership. I couldn't betray Midge's trust. The cold wind blew our hair in our eyes. I waited for the signal from Midge. She told me to take the stones and weeds in the wheelbarrow to the rubbish dump. 'Be ready to come to the hut.'

Each girl piled her rubbish on the path ready for collecting.

'Can I come with the wheelbarrow, Bonnie? Why can't I?'

'Midge chose me. Get on with the raking.'

Ula wanted to grow mustard and cress in shapes to come up next year. 'Hail Unicorn, Welcome Spring'. We had to explain that it wasn't possible. Phoebe refused to join in work outside. As head girl she chose to remain apart. Gubgub was kind, comforting the little ones if they scratched themselves on brambles, her red hair bright in the cold air. The school relied on the prefects and monitors, the Gee sisters looked so tired. I longed to tell Ula my secret, it would make her happy. Midge was coming, I could hear the barrow wheels. She paused by each girl. The frost-stiffened sods of earth and grass were piled into the barrow with the leaves and beech-nut casings. Midge was breathing hard. I took one handle of the barrow and we moved off down the path. We tipped it on to the rubbish dump. Now was the time for the hut.

'Don't make a sound, Bonnie, I'm warning you.'

I felt the warmth of her breath. Her cheek had a mud smear, her slitty eyes gleamed. Remember, Bonnie, not a sound.

I smell the beloved and unmistakable smell of mouse again. The cage is empty, no mouse to welcome us. We push our faces closer, listening, we hold our breath, it's too wonderful to believe. Tiny rustlings, silence and our breathing, tiny squeakings, silence again. Listen to the rustling and squeaking of motherhood.

'They're born. Born at last.'

We felt proud as if we'd worked a miracle; no midwife could have felt more joy. The mother had no time to run out and greet us, she had her family, her destiny for which she'd been born. We didn't speak again, we left food and crept away. What we felt must be holy rapture.

'Why were you so long, Bonnie? Your face is red. Are you cold?'

'It's the wind, stupid. Will it be lunchtime soon?'

My sisters were still squatting by their allotments. A

fresh gust of wind blew grit over us. Tor had always longed for a pet. Midge was my benefactress, she knew our secrets. Why couldn't my sisters find their own friends? Tor was too dependent, too clinging, too silent. Did proper mothers feel as I did, bored with their children, stuck with them, wanting to get away from them? How irritating they were, looking and questioning. I'd never have real children. I wouldn't marry until I was old.

Tor had been quick to learn the school jargon but she never used it. She only spoke to Ula and me. She had her precious diary to scribble in, that was all she wanted. I couldn't remember her laughing for months. Ula was perky, she could tell the time now, they both deserved normal fun. I didn't want them bothering when I was thinking of the mouse family. I could have smacked their faces for two pins.

It was Saturday, we did no lessons, just gardening or hanging about. There was no recreation room, just the form room. We sat at our desks at night. Midge lent me *The Study and Care of Rodents*. It became my Bible. I sat learning it while the rest gossiped or combed their hair. The Gee sisters were spending more and more time in their rooms beyond the conservatory. We did as we pleased, even eating supper at our desks. Gumm did less cooking now, often just sandwiches and perhaps some plain biscuits which we washed down with tea. My period was an important landmark in life for me. Finding the mice had brought me joy.

Miss Gee continued to pray for the war effort. Miss Patrice exhorted us to dig for victory and to save for the brave. The war was quite important and interesting for grown-up people to worry about. What mattered most was my sisters and me.

'Midge, I'll write to Mamma again. This time I will ask her. The babies must have everything they need.'

The form room door opened. Phoebe stood there.

'Hullo everyone. He's here, he's come to fetch me. My brother came. We're off for the weekend.'

I only glimpsed his face and hair the colour of pale string, like Phoebe's. '*A bientôt*,' Phoebe murmured.

The girls giggled with jealousy and excitement. So handsome, so debonair. Lucky Phoebe, she was the prettiest and most favoured, off now for celebrations at the Black Lion Hotel. We all envied her more than somewhat, it was swoon-making. We were stuck here with just old Gumm.

# *SIX*

---

We ate our supper sandwiches and speculated. Was Phoebe drinking champagne or cocktails, eating roast duck with orange segments by the light of candles? Was she discussing the war? Would her brother tell of his regiment's destination? We had seen his photograph, now we had seen the man. He was real and wonderful, he had her languid expression, her long-fingered hands. What would we not have given to be in her place? Gubgub spoke with yearning of smoked salmon and tiny peas. Midge liked lamb hash with carrots. Everyone had a favourite dish except Tor who didn't join in. Ula liked rock cakes made with jam in the centre. I liked hearing about food as we ate our frugal meal. I had never drunk alcohol except for some sherry once, when Bruno had died. I had only eaten in a restaurant once, that time with Mamma in London. I had never been close to anyone in love except the couple at the next table who had the diamond ring. I would always think of Mamma when I heard the dream song or smelled roses. I even thought of her when a spoon clinked.

'Midge, do you know a song called "When I grow too old to dream"?'

She said she did, it was rather sad. We discussed songs

59

then. There was one called the Umbrella song on a record. Barbie had a gramophone though it was broken. You had to start winding the handle as soon as the tune started, otherwise it wavered and wailed and became unrecognizable. If you wound without stopping you risked breaking the spring inside. Barbie didn't mind lending the gramophone but she stayed near it, her tiny arm working the handle like a piston. You got the idea of the tune in spite of the distortion; it was something to do besides talk. No one wanted to think about war news, though seeing Phoebe's brother made it all more real. He was the only soldier I knew by name, though I had barely got a glimpse of him. Mamma probably knew a lot of soldiers now. Miss Gee didn't mind Phoebe going out. Her brother was one of the fighting forces for whom she daily prayed. I thought of Phoebe lying under a black silk eiderdown printed with peonies in a room in the Black Lion Hotel while we slept in two rows here. Barbie was given to snoring, Ula moaned and ground her grey teeth. How would I manage my mouse at Christmas time when my sisters and I were alone? It would be grown and active by then. I longed to feel its whiskers, its slender tail curving my wrist. The claws of a mouse felt ecstatic. Grown-ups missed a lot by regarding them as pests.

'I've never had champagne,' Ula said boastfully. 'I know about whisky, of course. There's poteen too, that's illegal.'

Carried away she added that she wouldn't mind a night in a hotel, it would make a pleasant change. Gubgub said sharply that she was just a bumptious little child too much given to showing off. Midge, the peacemaker, said they didn't have alcohol in their home, that it made you sleepy and rude. Each child in her family had certain tasks, they had no servants like the other girls here. Sending Midge to this school was a sacrifice for her parents and they were not satisfied. Midge wasn't learning enough. Unless the situation improved they had written to say she must leave. I had never seen Mamma holding a duster or boiling water. We had had our governess and nurse and our cook. The more I heard about Midge's home the lovelier it sounded, especially at Christmas time. I supposed that our house would be full of soldiers now. Would they respect Mamma's chintz furnishings? Would generals sleep in our beds?

'Let's put the Umbrella song on again, may we, Barbie? I'll wind it, let me.'

'Can I see your book, Bonnie? What's it about? Mice? How *sweet*.'

'Anyone want to play noughts and crosses? This French waiter said noughts and *kisses*, my dear.'

'Let me wind, Barbie, you're too little.'

'Same to you with double knobs on.'

We missed Phoebe. We expected to see her pale, half-blind stare again in the doorway, to hear her sarcastic drawl. I had a dream that night of furless rats and mice gnawing each other; the rats had long red teeth and sightless eyes.

'You blame Ula for making a noise, Bonnie. You were moaning in your sleep just like her.'

All three of us had awful dreams sometimes. We couldn't climb into each other's beds for comfort, you couldn't do that at school. I thought of Phoebe again to help the dream to fade. Was she sleeping under the peony eiderdown or swaying to a jazz band in her high heels and her bra. She didn't mind having no real home or parents. Joining the army was her sole goal.

I would choose a white mouse if there was one, with peaceful, pale pink eyes.

On Monday morning Miss Gee spoke through grim lips from her dais. We sang no hymn, prayed no prayer for the war effort, she had important news that would affect us all. She paused, holding her ruler as if for strength. Had something happened to Phoebe? She hadn't returned last

61

night. Miss Gee had had a visit from the local billeting officer. It seemed there was a problem with some children evacuated from London who had failed to settle in foster homes. Local householders in the town were hurt and uneasy; the children wouldn't respond to care, their manners were rude and disruptive. As our school was not carrying the full number of pupils, Miss Gee had no alternative but to offer a sanctuary. No patriot could refuse this call. The country needed us, she and Miss Patrice had agreed. The children would arrive shortly. There was silence. Miss Gee stood like a sentry on duty. Any questions, girls?

'Will they do lessons with us, Miss Gee?' Midge asked.

The strange children would continue their studies in the town. Their own teacher had come with them from Clerkenwell, a person used to their ways. 'We are short of staff here, don't forget, Margaret.'

'I'd like them to learn with us. Our lessons are sometimes ...'

'Ula, put your hand up before you speak, please. The children will sleep here only.'

Their weekends would be spent at school. It would be fresh opportunity for patriotism. Our land called, we would give up our strength and our beds. This was a new meaning of lending to defend. She had not anticipated Magnolia House becoming a refuge for less privileged children. Midge asked where they would sleep. Would they obey the prefects and monitors?

Miss Gee made it clear that the strangers must submit to our school regulations while under its roof. We must realize that they would be unfamiliar with etiquette and *savoir-faire*. Elegance and inner grace would be unknown qualities. We must be patient. Any questions?

Ula put up her hand. 'Will they have fleas?'

The girls tittered. I hated Ula again for making herself so conspicuous. I admired her too. I didn't want any strange

62

children invading us just when school was getting better. They might smell or steal my watch. I put my own hand up.

'How many children, Miss Gee? How long will they be here?'

'That is not for you to question, Bona. This is war.'

War was silly. Loving your country was silly. No one asked us if we wanted to fight or take in strangers. Old Gumm was upset this morning, the toast was uneatable.

Miss Patrice was in a state of exhilaration. London children held no threat for her, she welcomed the challenge. This was her opportunity to assume leadership from her sister. Miss Gee was feeling her age. Miss Patrice wore her thin locks flattened into a dark-coloured bandeau like a little soft crown. These strange children were our war bonus, she said earnestly, a chance for each one of us to shine. She would like to offer a prize to the most helpful Magnolia girl. The strangers would be homesick, we must welcome them with arms opened wide. They might not be used to English properly expressed; we must talk clearly and slowly. Their manners might seem quaint, their hygiene less than adequate.

'Do you mean they don't wash?'

Miss Patrice didn't rebuke Ula for her practical questions. Remember that we were asked to save fuel. Share with those less fortunate. Poor Gumm would be even busier. She counted on her Magnolias to help both indoors and out.

I thought that the two old ladies and the elderly gardener already had enough to do. Miss Gee had been silly to accept.

'Cockneys are renowned for their courage and their humour, girls. Instead of doubting, worrying and wondering, let us pull with a will and smile.'

She hoped that we would share our good fortune with enthusiasm. She would like us to go to our allotments now and start sectioning them into halves. We would welcome the strangers with a gift of land.

There was no sign of Phoebe. The two sisters were too perturbed to notice she was still gone. We grumbled as we put on our raincoats. Why should we share our gardens? I liked having my sisters near, without strangers listening to us. Miss Patrice gave us wooden stakes and lengths of string. Measure and mark out portions for the strangers. Generosity was better than gold. Drive the stakes, wind the string, make ready the precious soil. Land was heritage, give it freely. Share and care, girls, care and share.

Ula had broken a plate at supper. She had collected the china pieces to make an edge for our plots. I missed the croquet lawn, the molehills, croquet hoops and leaves. The cold brown earth looked unfriendly, with the stakes, string and broken china. I cut Ula's string with a pruning knife, remembering her fear of knives. Miss Patrice patrolled the path as we laboured, her rubber soles quick with joy. I felt under my sleeve for Mamma's gift. I would always wear it to be on the safe side. The Clerkenwells might be light-fingered, they might hate us and do us harm. I didn't know what heritage meant. I guessed that Tor was feeling as I did, excited, curious and annoyed.

'They won't be sharing lessons with us, Tor. At least we can be thankful for that.'

Miss Patrice heard me. She stood still, her fudge-col-oured eyes looked sad under her little cloth crown. Shar-ing was caring, Bonnie, remember that, the strangers were far from their homes. We had so much here, practise *noblesse oblige*, consider others. 'Yes, girls, I am speaking of love. This is your chance to practise charity.'

We tittered and felt uneasy, she embarrassed us with her lectures. Generosity, patriotism, sharing and caring. Same to you with double knobs on, go away, leave us alone. Her face had a melted look in the cold weather, her eyes were liquid with zeal, her nostrils gleamed. She said that with Christmas approaching some of us might like to ask a stranger home with us.

'Does that mean they won't go back to Clerkenwell for the holiday?' I asked sharply. Would our holiday plans be upset? There was my mouse to consider now, as well as my sisters. How Miss Patrice's face irritated me. How silly all the girls looked kneeling by their plots. Where was Midge with the barrow?

Then she appeared wheeling it carefully past the potting sheds, but she wasn't looking at me but behind me.

I turned. A group of girls appeared round the school. These must be the Clerkenwells arriving before we'd had time to imagine what they'd be like. What struck me was that they looked annoyed.

They'd been turned out of their town billets without being consulted. They looked shabby but far from abject. Their coats were too short and tight under the armpits, they wore plimsolls or sad-looking shoes. They stared back at us with knowing eyes. A bus had brought them from their school in the town with their luggage. The girl in front had a red beret. Her coat didn't button. I saw a row of little warty spots round her neck like a necklace. She took her hands from her pockets. Her dirt-rimmed nails had flaking red polish on them. Her wrists were bony and she wore lipstick. My sisters and I were still kneeling with stakes and string in our hands.

'What you lot doing? This a prayer meeting?'

'Did you see our unicorn? You should have come in by the front door, not the side.'

'Be quiet, Ula. That's one of our headmistresses, Miss Patrice, over there.'

Miss Patrice rushed forward, her lashes damp with welcome.

'Cordial greetings, we extend our welcome. I speak on behalf of us all.'

65

'Yeh? Ta. Where's the other head lady? The old one.'

Miss Patrice explained that Miss Gee was feeling tired. That we were preparing and dividing our plots to give our guests as a welcome. Working in pairs we would till and cull, dig for victory, lend to defend. We offered them land.

'What, grubbing in this cold? No ta.'

Miss Patrice blinked. We were preparing the soil for spring vegetables, though the little ones might be allowed flowers. A few button daisies or pansies perhaps, but culinary produce was our aim.

'Don't fancy vedges. Other than tin peas.'

The rest closed behind her in a sleazy-coated scowling band.

'Well well, put out the flags,' drawled Phoebe's familiar voice. She was back with her coat round her shoulders like a cloak, her hat brim making a halo round the back of her head. Our queen had returned from her weekend at the Black Lion. The visitors sniffed, unimpressed by Phoebe's soft silk stockings, her shoes with little heels. Their own socks or laddered cotton stockings creasing into their lamentable shoes didn't shame them. Phoebe was too big for her boots.

'Phoebe, child. You are back in time to welcome our London guests.'

'London guests? *Zut alors.*'

# SEVEN

Phoebe didn't ask why they were here; she assumed that the Gee sisters were mad as usual. She should have stayed at the Black Lion with her soldier brother. She must be missing him. It was war and he had gone. I would have been happy for her to turn to me for consolation. I would heal her broken heart. The strangers were not impressed. She was just another toffee-nosed cow with more swank than sense. The Magnolia girls rose from their cramped positions. The hems of our raincoats were damp, our Wellingtons were smeared with soil. I wiped my hands on my hanky. Miss Patrice said, adjusting her bandeau, that Phoebe should have been here a moment sooner, in time for the welcome. Phoebe shrugged; the party of cockneys were of no interest.

'What's that animal in front on the gatepost?' The girl in the red beret seemed to be their spokesman.

'Our unicorn, dear, our mascot. The unicorn is a symbol of protection.'

'You mean bombs and that?'

Miss Patrice explained the legend about the unicorn protecting the other animals, thus it was held in high esteem. By dipping its horn into poisoned waters they were made safe. The girl in the beret sniffed.

'Figuratively speaking, my dear. The beast is hetero-geneous. Did you notice the lion's tail? It is an aggregate of other animals. It has elephant's feet.'

'Can't say I did. Where are our beds? We got to get our things straight.'

Miss Patrice hoped that their stay here would be com-panionable. Would each of them like to choose a Magnolia girl to be her guide and mentor?

'Guide? Eh?'

'We want you to look on our girls as godmothers or aunties. Come girlies, choose a chum.'

'You joking? We got to find our beds. We got to get back to school. Oh all right, I'll have you.'

The beret girl walked over to Phoebe who yawned in her face. They walked ahead back inside the school. The rest of us followed. Miss Patrice ought to have warned us; we didn't feel godmotherly or even friendly towards these children. I supposed we would have to give in. But Midge had other views.

'I don't want to be anyone's godmother, thank you Miss Patrice. Being head girl is quite enough.'

And she was in charge of the grounds now that Gumm was indoors all day. She wanted to make it clear that Bonnie was her second-in-command outside. Just Bonnie, no one else.

I would do anything for Midge. I would heave rocks to the rubbish dump single-handed, I would clean the pot-ting sheds, render the incinerator odourless as long as our mice were safe.

By the time we were back in the dormitory Phoebe and the girl in the beret whose name was Red had arranged to sleep next to each other. The other five could choose to sleep in either dormitory. Red and Phoebe drew the curtains round their beds at the far end, away from the clank of the basins and the gurgle of the bath plugs. Red thumped her case down. 'Tell me all,' I heard Phoebe say. They whispered, occasionally they laughed. Red's laughter was snickering; Phoebe laughed almost soundlessly, on an indrawn breath with her lips pulled into a square. In no time they had become an exclusive society with a membership of two.

The school felt different, already the smell had changed. Keatings powder, greasy hair and plimsolls took over from talcum powder, toothpaste and new clothes. Midge was sitting on her bed reading, with her hair hanging over her face. Had Phoebe forgotten her now that she'd found Red. Midge was too proud to show that she cared.

The other strangers were slow to speak. We all strained to hear what Phoebe and Red were saying. A smell of vanilla essence seemed to creep through their curtains. It was Red's perfume. Her boyfriend liked it. It lingered on your clothes. The Magnolia girls were alerted; none of them spoke openly of boys. They had crushes on waiters they'd seen on their holidays, they giggled over 'you-know-who', they swooned at the names of each other's brothers. Their 'you-know-whos' didn't exist. Red made the word boyfriend sound thrilling and wicked. Midge thought all that sort of thing absurd. Red was a novelty; we were agog.

Miss Patrice had spoken to the billeting officer about the strangers' health records. She needed their London addresses. Had she noted Red's warty looking spots? I tried to peer through the gap in the curtains. Red was using a disgusting puff on her neck. She had an almost lipless mouth. Phoebe was holding Red's tin compact as if it were platinum. Red, with her boyfriend and vanilla perfume, engrossed her. She saw me watching and closed the curtains. The other visitors tipped their cases on to their beds as we had done when we arrived. Their cases were cardboard, split and broken, they had threaded the strings of their gas mask cases through the handles. The clothes in the cases looked like rags washed to no colour. A girl kept sneezing and coughing. She wiped her eyes on a piece of torn vest. Another girl gave her a piece of cough candy with paper sticking to it. They found a comic and started to read, their mouths making sucking sounds between the coughs and sneezes.

'Can I look?' Ula asked.

The comic looked exciting and colourful, you could understand without needing to read. Ula was used to film magazines but we'd never had comics. Tor had gone out, probably to the form room. The visitors showed no interest in our school. They didn't require godmothers or friendship, they needed to get back to their own school. They looked at our bath cubicles with dislike and suspicion. Too much hot water made you soft in the head.

'Now, girlies, settling comfortably?'

Miss Patrice was busy and happy. Had everyone chosen a fairy godmother? Where was Phoebe, her trusted head girl? She cleared her throat. Sharing cubicles was not encouraged here. The visitors would soon learn our ways. We aimed at grace and inner elegance. Magnolia House was democratic, we worked toward the common good. Now, did everyone understand the itinerary. Each weekday the bus would take them to their school in the town. On their return to Magnolia supper would be waiting. Their weekends would be spent here. The Clerkenwells and the Magnolias would be expected to share the chores, putting shoulders to the wheel. The everyday running of the school would fall largely on the girls. Both teaching and domestic staff were reduced owing to the war.

'No more servants to do your work, diddums?' Red didn't bother to lower her voice.

Miss Patrice suggested that we might like to work in teams. What about Maggies and Clerkies? Red made a face of nausea. She snatched her gas mask and went downstairs. No one was interested in team spirits, democracy or elegance. Miss Patrice stood at the top of the stairs and called down. 'Pride, girlies. I'm talking about pride. In yourselves, in the school, in England.'

Red looked back. 'Look, Miss, we need more pillows, we none of us can sleep flat. We ain't dirty, we don't need baths. Pillows.'

Miss Patrice had observed their bad posture, their congested breathing and coughs. One pillow aided deportment. Bad posture and poor hygiene took toll.

Phoebe yawned again. She liked lounging on pillows in preference to fresh air and gardening. Also she liked deep scented baths. If she paired off with Red I could spend more time with Midge. Midge would turn to me. She had spoken again of her parents' dissatisfaction with the school. She was learning nothing. She wanted to study animal ailments, she wanted to be a vet. She was different from Phoebe who just wanted a good time in the army. Midge must have a career, she mustn't waste her time. A veterinary training took years; all her books were about animals. She had sympathy for people. She was quite concerned about the Gee sisters. The war was a burden for the elderly.

That evening the visitors glared at the undercooked rice pudding. The sausages had been raw. They noted the way we held our cutlery, the way we sipped water without gulping. Nothing impressed them. They pushed their plates aside.

'Do you always eat this type of food? I wouldn't give it to my dog.'

'Where is your dog, Red?'

'With Mum and Dad, of course. Clerkenwell.'

Red was used to proper teas in the kitchen; good strong tea, not this dishlap. Thick bread with chips. Sundays in Clerkenwell they ate jellied eels and mash. This rice pudden was raw. Phoebe agreed. Red was *absolument* correct, it was uneatable. She had another banana, she gave

71

half of it to Red. Old Gumm should be put out to grass. We had heard about her dinners with her uncle at his Mayfair club. She had had steak with her brother at the Black Lion.

'What do you do after this lot, then?'

'We read or we play Barbie's gramophone in the form room. The babies go to bed.'

'You got a grammie? Where?'

We explained about the broken spring and only owning one record. Red thought it was bad having no sitting room.

'Do you know the Umbrella Song, Red?'

'Course.'

'What about "Run Rabbit Run"?'

'And "South of the Border".'

'"Begin the Beguine", "Deep Purple", "Roll out the Barrel".'

We wanted Red to know that we knew the right tunes, were up to the minute with songs. She fiddled with her spoon, pinching her thin lips inwards. Her permed hair was like a bush beside Phoebe's flat locks. Both were stylish in different ways. Red called to Gumm. 'Hey, Hitler, you trying to poison us? This the best you can do?'

He turned away.

'Come on you lot. Leave Hitler to his slops.'

I hated Gumm being humiliated. He had done his best here for forty years. He must long to fight for his country with younger men rather than cook for impudent girls.

The form room seemed smaller now, filled with so many girls. The babies stayed up tonight. Barbie's gramophone was by the gas mask hooks. Phoebe had brought back a surprise from her weekend, a record of 'There's a Small Hotel'.

'And look, Tor. On the other side it's our song.'

She looked at me strangely, then turned away. Didn't she want to remember that happy tea in London, the cream cakes, Mamma's throaty voice, the couple with the diamond ring? She made me feel disloyal. I was spending too much time with Midge. I still loved her, she must realize that.

Red was impatient with slow tunes. Play something with a bit of life, not that waltzing slop. 'Come on, you twerps. Let's dance.' She and her lot were used to real dancing. Push up the speed, Barb, faster than that. Come on, Phoeeb, bugger the rest, let's do some dancing.

Phoebe's myopic eyes started to shine. Her brother danced formally, guiding his partners over the floors of nightclubs with practised hands. Red danced wildly. She needed a fast beat and room to move. She and Phoebe had already formed their private way of talking barely moving their lips, a secret language. Now they danced. They moved so fast their bodies seemed to whirl. Red pushed and pulled her, showing her. Don't be so stiff, move from the neck down, move the whole body, loosen your shoulders and knees. They touched, they broke away, rejoined and parted, every inch must be alive. You got it, Phoeeb, I'm learning you, it's easy if you let go. The record finished. They were panting. Red had learned from her boyfriend at home.

Ula wanted to know about the boyfriend. Wasn't Red a bit young?

'Never too old or too young, kiddo. Watch out, keep out of our way.'

They were off again. Ula looked serious. She felt uneasy about boyfriends because of the way our cook had gone off with men. We had met few men ourselves, few boys and were not used to having friends. Red's perfume and dancing gave an entry into a private and forbidden world of which we knew nothing. Scrawny, mean-lipped, spotty-necked Red knew about life. Ula stamped her shoes, sideways and forwards, sticking out her bottom. 'I'm dancing. Look at me.'

'Who you supposed to be? Charlie Chaplin?'

73

'Ula, don't try to show off.'

I snubbed her but I wanted to dance too. I wanted to dance better than Red and Phoebe, I wanted to outshine everyone here. They must watch me, not Red and Phoebe. Why should they get all the praise? I had tried the splits and got menstruation. Did you always pay for showing off? Ula went on jumping busily, showing her awful teeth. Phoebe and Red were leaping dervishes. The gramophone sounded like animal squeals. Phoebe our goddess and dirty Red were magical. 'Good old Phoeeb, not half bad. Come on, you lot, have a try.'

We joined in, trying to copy, moving the best way we could. The Clerkenwells were used to letting go in their playground and jumping in the London streets. They weren't self-conscious, they could dance without effort. The Magnolias were stiff and ill at ease. It was our turn now to be awkward, lacking grace, elegance and style. We had never seen or heard of this sort of dancing, it was very different from the waltz. Gubgub could dance the Gay Gordons and there was the Lambeth Walk. Midge took hold of Ula.

'Come on, Tor. Let's you and I try.'

She moved away from me like a stranger. I caught a whiff of her sweat. Why was she angry? Didn't she know I'd never forget her?

'Come on, Tor, let's try.'

'So kiss me my sweet, and so let us part, When I grow too old to dream, your love will live in my heart.'

'Wind the grammie, faster, faster, wind it quick, you bloodclot.'

I went stiff. What a disgusting word for Red to use in front of children. Then the light was turned off. It was easier in the darkness, you didn't feel so self-conscious. Horrible word. I felt Tor breathing, smelled her, felt her cold fingers in my hand. We heard leather shoes scuffling, plimsolls slithering, mufti dresses brushed the visitors'

74

rags. It was pitch-black, then gradually you could see shapes of dancers. I need you, Tor; nothing has changed, believe that. I promised Mamma that I'd look after you but I have to learn new things. The cockneys know things we've never heard of, swearing and dancing and boys. I want to be wise and kind like Midge. I want to stay a child but I've menstruated. I can't stay the same, I am older. Don't leave me, Tor, be the same.

Phoebe and Red shared the same bath. Midge didn't show that she cared. Sharing baths was worse than sharing beds or lavatories. Midge helped Ula fold her clothes. 'And we'll pull our beds close,' Phoebe said. With pillows touching they murmured their closed-lipped language, having splashed and tittered in the bath. Had they compared toe-nails, bust measurement and body hair, having left wet marks on the slatted mat? Red had a photograph of her boyfriend wearing battledress. We all wanted to see his gap-toothed smile and sleek hair combed straight back. Phoebe's brother was framed in silver. His bony jaw impressed us and his neat pale hair. Red looked at him, then kissed her own picture smackingly.

'Let me see, Red. Please?'

Ula wanted to know what ITALY in the corner meant. Was he Italian? Ula was beginning to read now.

'Blimey. Ed an Eyetye?' Red kissed her picture again. I Trust and Love You was what it meant. Phoebe jerked the curtains close round their beds, the bed springs creaked, they were alone. Red was filthy, the bathroom stank of her, she had spots and said disgusting words. She was only thirteen but we all wanted to listen to her, would like to be a little like her. Her life in Clerkenwell sounded better than our lives. She went to Saturday night pictures and the market with her mum. She could roller-skate, her dog was called Bony. Her dad came home shouting from the pub. They ate in the kitchen, the table had newspapers, they had winkles and meat pies from a stall.

Their parlour was kept for Christmas and birthdays. She missed that parlour and Sunday teas. Boys liked you to have tits in front and lipstick for kissing, they liked frizzy hair and hot perfume. Best of all they liked you alone. Imagining her home must be like watching a film, though we'd never been to one, except for one about bees making honey in our Town Hall. Red's home sounded so friendly, she'd never wanted to come away. When she married she wanted one kiddy and to live in Clerkenwell near her mum. They'd eat winkles and drink sodas while they gave eye to the kiddy. She didn't want to join in the war. Her dad was a fire fighter in the city, it was dangerous. Her mum and her and the kiddy would be sunny as larks. She wasn't like Phoebe, wanting to join up for travel and glamour. Red believed in family ties.

I didn't feel tired or sleepy. The war was horrid, the way it changed everyone's lives. We might never see Mamma again, but at least we'd met the Clerkenwells. My nipples hurt, I hated having pubic hair. Tor made me feel trapped and guilty. I envied Ula, still just a little child. She was sitting in bed rubbing on face cream. We didn't want to catch Red's spots.

Red was rude again in the morning. 'Look, chum, whatever they call you. We can't eat this slop. Worse than sick.'

Gumm looked at the porridge, then looked at her spots.

'Cook it yourself. I'm off.'

# EIGHT

'Not like that, Phoebe, you clot. You're burning it.'

'It should be well browned, Red. I had it once with my uncle.'

'Bugger your uncle, he ain't here. They can put jam on it.'

'Not *jam*, Red, this is a savoury.'

Ula pushed in. 'I love jam, Red. Jam on fried bread is nice.'

'No one asked you, kiddo. Phoeeb and I are the cooks.'

Phoebe ran her hand through her fringe. She let Red take her place at the stove.

'Red, what does "copulation" mean?'

'You'll cop it if you get in my way. Phoeeb you're burning it.'

School supper was called tea now. Phoebe and Red ruled the kitchen, smoky now with burning fat. Midge was cleaning potatoes in the corner. Gumm had kept his word and left.

Red said his food was dangerous, he'd better not show his face. Miss Patrice's sallow face had lengthened. A faithful retainer had been insulted. We were now without paid help. She had pleaded in vain. Gumm was unused to rudeness, he would not change his mind. She didn't wish to lay blame on one person, the school must bear the shame collectively. A servant had been treated inelegantly. Her sister had been made ill. Now Miss Patrice took morning assembly alone.

'What is wrong with Miss Gee, please?'

She was prone to stomach upsets, any friction could set it off.

'Told you. Poison,' Red muttered.

Miss Patrice still wore her bandeau. It looked careless, her hair pushed it to one side. She looked worn out. She was now asking the school for further endeavours. Would we cook as well as keeping the premises tidy? She looked at Red, a hint of coldness in her fudge-coloured eyes, their lids pink now as if from crying. Because of Red we must all pay the price. Red looked back at her and gave her snickering laugh. She had no time for old people, not a lot of time for these toffee-nosed girls, except, of course, old Phoeeb. But this school was better than staying in those billets; she could be with her mates each night as well as at school, plus she'd met and chummed with Phoeeb.

'And so, girls, prefects and monitors will be our leaders in the absence of domestic and academic staff, all of whom have gone to serve. Any questions?'

'What's the pay?' Red called.

Phoebe said that she and Red would take over the cooking. Midge and I were assigned all garden duties and outside control. Red complained about the Gees' meanness. They were saving wages, we should get paid for the work.

Each morning she and Phoebe rose before the rest, to make toast. Tea was made in a large enamel pot with milk and sugar added. They enjoyed themselves in the kitchen, muttering their rapid talk. Midge and I helped prepare vegetables. Red said she felt like shopping the Gees to the government. They were profiteering from this war, two

78

old spivs.

Supper was always late. They argued over menus. Red yearned for whelks and jellied eels, Phoebe for pheasant or jugged hare, all impossible. They didn't know how to cook in any case. They agreed that time spent in cooking should be as short as possible, they liked dancing together best.

The larder had been a shock. Gumm had either stolen the rations or not ordered any. The shelves were bare and dirty. Rice and sugar jars were empty, a few eggs in a bowl were bad. There was nothing under the china cheese cover. There was a paper sack of porridge, some old bread in a bin. In the refrigerator was a parcel of sausages; their shiny red skins smelled. A spider ran round the tea packet. The baker said that he'd been instructed to leave old bread. A few minutes in a hot oven under a damp cloth freshened it. Red said her mum did that but you'd expect fresh bread in this place. Two spivs, nothing less nor more. Red liked bread cut into a bowl with milk and some sugar, so we had that often now. With Phoeeb's money and brains Red thought she should know more about cooking.

'Not like that, you clot. Too many servants has made you helpless.'

'I can't help it, Red. I've had no opportunity.'

'Diddums, you're getting it now.'

The Clerkenwells hadn't met Miss Gee yet, still in her room with her stomach complaint, waited on by Miss Patrice. Her walk had lost its bounce, her hair grew droopier. She spoke with less vigour about patriotism and inner elegance, the country's needs, the danger of careless talk. 'Thrift, girls, I urge you to practise thrift.'

The Clerkenwells were unimpressed by her, nor did they feel curiosity about Miss Gee. They still missed Clerkenwell.

The evenings were our happiest times. With tea eaten

we went back to the form room. Without our uniforms our behaviour seemed to change. The differences in speech and manners became less obvious. We became less separate, our backgrounds didn't count. Without grown-ups to bother us, the war and its silly rules didn't count either. What mattered was dancing to the gramophone.

'Not that way, Phoeeb. Gas is too high.'

Slices of bread and hot fat hissed as Red dumped the contents of the frying pan into the rubbish bucket. A lump of lard melted into a cabbage leaf.

'I'll empty it. Can I?'

'You again, Ula?'

'Let her, Phoebe. She likes helping.'

Ula liked emptying and tidying. Red didn't want kids under her feet. She let Ula take the bucket to the back door. She wanted to go on gossiping with Phoeeb.

I spent more time in Midge's company. The winter had set in, there was still a little work to do. The paths must be kept tidy, the potting sheds kept neat. There was the incinerator and rubbish dump to see to. We spent hours with the mouse family, they led such happy lives. The babies were out of their nest now but couldn't be handled. There was the white one of my dreams, there was a black one with a slightly snouty nose. I worried about the thin pitiful one that trembled. I could have two if I wanted, Midge said, but they'd have to be the same sex. She was so knowledgeable and expert, lifting the young by their tails. They needed a protein and carbohydrate diet. Mice were prone to virus infections, salmonellosis, Tyzzer's disease. With proper care they could live for three years or more. I memorized her learned veterinary information. I would be nearly fifteen when they died.

We cleaned the cage, having removed the nesting box; we discussed names for the mice. The rubbish and incinerator-burning took place on Sundays when the girls were supposed to be visiting the high church in the town. A bus called for the churchgoers but no one used it, preferring to stay in bed, eating toast and talking about their lives. We learned more about the Clerkenwells than they did about us; their opinion of posh people was low. Our toffee-nosed parents couldn't manage without servants. It was a shock to find no servants here and no staff. The school they went to in the town was better off. The town children were taught proper lessons and given a proper lunch. They could do easy algebra and knew the rivers and capital cities of the world. The Magnolias were freaks from freakish homes in their opinion, not knowing much and showing off. They remembered Clerkenwell with nostalgia. Cosy oil fires were better than cool heating pipes. To sit round a lit gas oven with plates warming or clothes airing was companionable. They liked being squashed together in one bed. They liked Joe Loss and Henry Hall on the wireless. They liked Roy Rogers and the *Beano* and chips. Where was the pub or the chip shop? This place was poverty-stricken, though we let on to be posh.

Red's dad being in the Fire Service meant he earned more than some of them. Red had a three-piece suite in their parlour with a rimless mirror over the fire. They had a shiny coal scuttle. Her mum made suet puddings called Spotted Dick. These old teacher sisters were mad in the head and mean with it. Red's dog did better. Once we had the grammie going in the evening, it was all right.

She and Phoebe slapped the bread slices on to plates, ladling the jam on.

'Hurry, you lot. Time for tea.'

We heard the click and tap of knives and spoons in the dining room, we heard Ula boasting again. She liked setting tables, she liked folding tableclothes, she liked sounding the bell outside.

As the weeks passed our appearance changed as well as

81

our voices. Red started a fashion for curling our hair. She used lead strips covered with stocking silk to wind round small strands of hair, using six for her fringe alone. Her wrists were less thin in spite of the diet, her spots didn't seem quite so bright. Frizzed hair might suit me, my hair was longer now. There were no more indoor games or Biblical Tableau practice. The hymn singing and praying stopped too. Miss Patrice asked if the head girls would conduct assembly; we forgot the end of term pageant. We shared our things increasingly with the Clerkenwells who had to dress in the weekdays for their school. They wore our uniforms when they fancied, there was no one to mend or launder, our clothes became grubby and frayed. We often kept our pyjamas on in the daytime, though we still liked bathing. So did Red.

The cupboards and drawers became clothes pools. You took out what you liked to put on, throwing things anywhere at night. We liked wearing the visitors' rings and bracelets that left green marks on your skin. Red let some of us use her lipstick. Sharing was interesting, it made a change. The important event each night was the dancing, always ending up in the dark.

The little ones went to bed when they wanted, our sweating bodies writhed. We went on until our legs ached, just like a real London dance palace. I trusted the Clerkenwells now. I was learning two important new subjects, how to dance and look after mice. Phoebe's brother sent more records. The dream song was left aside. I would never forget it, I would always love it. Mamma hadn't written. Red got a tin watch from her boyfriend. It wouldn't tick, though she wound and wound. What you could do mattered more than what you had. Red was proud of herself.

''Course, if you got the army occupying you got no worries.'

'What do you mean, Red?'

She said they paid a lot to use your house in wartime, a wonder the Gee sisters didn't let this place. It wasn't a proper school, not what she'd expected. Her mum would be disgusted if she saw. Catch her stopping a minute longer than she had to. Her boyfriend Ed had put in for Christmas leave. Clerkenwell was all right at Christmas, they knew how to do things right.

'You shouldn't go back to London. You might get bombed. Don't.'

'You joking? Try and stop me. My mum's there besides. Not everyone runs away, scaredy cat.'

'My oh my,' Phoebe sighed.

They were best friends but I think Phoebe envied her. An officer brother wasn't like a soldier who trusted and loved you. No one was bored with Red around. It was rare now to hear anyone say 'Catch me ere I swoon' or 'more than somewhat'. There were no gasps or French catchwords now. The Magnolias didn't drop their aitches (except for Ula sometimes) but vowel sounds were less pure, consonants less ringing. Our favourite supper became boiled eggs.

I liked listening to the sounds in the dining room when eggs were eaten, the chip of shells, the shells being dropped. I liked the tapping of spoons, the smashing of shells when they were empty. The Magnolias stopped slicing the tops off, we peeled the eggs like buns, ate them in our hands greedily. Crumbs fell from our fingers, our teeth became crusted with yolk. Eat quickly, never mind table manners, we mustn't waste good dancing time.

'What about washing up?'

'Bugger the dishes, they can wait.'

The magic movement and music took over, we were united, without difference of background, money or class. There was joy in moving to music, changing partners in the dark. Barbie or Ula called when it was time to change, switching the light out; you left your partner, you found someone else. You pushed, you giggled, you stumbled, you must guess before the lights went on. The desks were outside in the passage now, we'd stopped using them. The music screeched. Lights out. Change. I liked dancing with Ula, she moved jauntily, in a funny hopping kind of way. Her bones felt light and brittle. I asked if she was happy since the Clerkenwells had come.

'I'm usually happy. It's Tor, Bonnie. She cries sometimes. She bites her nails, she never used to. And she ...'

'Lights out. Close your eyes. Change.'

'Midge. It's you.'

'Bonnie, I've got something to tell you. I had a letter. I'm leaving.'

'What?'

'I'm leaving at Christmas.'

'You can't. You mustn't, Midge.'

'It's true. They've found another school for me. They're coming for the pageant.'

'Who will be head garden prefect? The mice. Midge, don't leave me.'

'You must choose someone to help you. You'll be in charge.'

Midge must have a better education, she mustn't waste time here. The war would end one day, she wanted to be a vet. She'd need biology, Latin, maths, chemistry, she was learning nothing here.

'The others are happy here. Phoebe and Gubgub.'

'They're different, they're not serious, you and I are.'

Some people never acquired ambition. This school was useless if you aimed high. She had a goal, nothing would prevent her, she would become a vet or die.

My only goal so far was to care for my sisters, and keep Midge's friendship and respect. Without her the rubbish disposal would be a misery, the incinerator a gruesome task. I needed her advice on mousekeeping, I needed her

84

for bodily matters. I had no one to rely on. Midge you can't go.

'Tor is unhappy. You must ask her, Bonnie. She's your sister, ask her to help.'

# NINE

'Bonnie, dearest. Too sad to have been so remiss. It's tragic that I cannot attend your pageant but we'll think of each other.'

I read Mamma's letter to my sisters. The Magnolia girls would have parents or relatives for the pageant, but not the Clerkenwells whose parents couldn't afford the fare from London. Phoebe hoped for her brother, Red hoped for her boyfriend. Planning and hoping for the soldiers strengthened their bond. Midge would leave after the pageant. I had been hoping that Mamma might meet Midge, my first friend and my guide.

We had forgotten about the pageant. There was little time now for rehearsals. The tableaux depicting prophets and wise men of the Old Testament would be changed to something simpler. We decided on Bible Beasts. We were engrossed in dancing and cooking. Only Ula, who helped Barbie with food for the Gee sisters, had remembered the pageant when she'd seen Miss Gee's ill-looking, stone-coloured face. We heard about the dying cheeseplant in the conservatory and the cold uncomfortable rooms the sisters had. The sisters picked at their food and Miss Patrice had lost weight.

87

The blackboard had no timetable now, there were no desks in the form room. But we could all read, Ula too. Tor had helped her, as once she used to help me. Phoebe had appointed herself our headmistress, with Red her second-in-command. They strode about in their mixed-up clothing. Phoebe's jewellery looked pretty on Red, the Magnolia uniform fitted her. We put the Gee sisters out of our mind; patriotism and England's future mattered less than comics, dancing and curling our hair. *Savoir-faire*, inner elegance and grace stayed beyond the conservatory. Each night the Magnolias were impatient for the Clerkenwell school bus to return from the town, the fun could start then.

One evening when I was waiting at the gate for the bus I felt that I was being watched. I touched the stone unicorn's shoulder for confidence. I shouldn't be in front of the school in my pyjamas. I had lead curling pins in my hair. Was that Miss Gee's face behind the magnolia branches where I and my sisters had waited once? Her face looked twisted and contorted, she seemed to be wringing her hands. I blinked. She was gone.

No one minded Midge barring them from the garden; it was so cold now, our secret mice were safe. Phoebe and Red barred everyone from the kitchen. Girls tended to pair off in twos. Tor was alone a lot. I couldn't help it. I would make it up to her when I could. We had come to meet other girls as well as to be educated; I needed and loved Midge. The cage must be cleaned daily, the mice grew quickly. We let them run through our fingers, round our wrists, up into our hair, leaving their sweet mousey scent behind. Tor often looked at me strangely, though I hadn't seen her cry.

The day of the pageant was getting closer. The animal idea came from Midge. As her father was a rector she knew her Bible; there were all kinds of Bible beasts. We wanted to retain the religious theme from consideration for Miss Gee, this being a church school. There were the Gadarene swine who rushed down a cliff, killing themselves, there were sheep and other farm animals round the manger. Camels, sparrows, donkeys, lions, peacocks, every kind of animal was mentioned somewhere. They were nicer than people, more interesting to act.

'We must have dancing, Midge, after all our practice.'

Red suggested the animals in the ark. Two by two we would dance into it; we would continue to dance inside. The animals would need exercise and amusement after getting so wet in the flood. Phoebe and Red would be Mr and Mrs Noah looking after us. Everyone wanted to be the best animals, elephants, monkeys or bears. It was decided to draw lots from slips of paper. You drew your animal and found your mate. Ula looked sad, what about the singing? She'd looked forward to leading the choir.

'No choir,' Phoebe dictated. The show must be simple, without complications. If singing was needed the audience could be the choir. There was to be nothing churchy or high-minded about the evening, the show would be short and sweet. Those who liked could make masks and tails for our animal dancing. Come on, everyone, draw lots now.

Midge picked first, she drew a mouse. I was next, another mouse. We were still partners, there was no one I'd rather dance with. We'd played with the mice all that day. Gubgub and Barbie were the ark's two pigs. Tor was a goat, the coughing girl was her partner, her name was Pegeen. For the first time I can remember Tor objected. She'd like to partner Ula. Couldn't she change? Pegeen coughed angrily. She didn't want to be a goat either, not with Tor.

'Can't change. Stick to the rules, you bloodclot.'

Tor blushed. I hated Red for calling her that name.

Ula was left out, we were an odd number. She was cheerful about it, didn't mind being in the ark on her own.

Was there an animal that sang?

'Let her be a unicorn.'

'Like the one outside. Yes.'

'There's no such animal. There couldn't be.'

'It's mentioned in the Bible often. What about psalm twenty-two?' Midge said the unicorn was famous, talked and written of but never seen. There were legends from many countries, China, India, Armenia, all had stories. The unicorn was beloved and venerated but never captured though hunters set traps with cunning and guile.

'Listen to the preacher's daughter. Swallowed a Bible lately?'

'Shut up, Red. Midge is going to be a vet.'

'Couldn't Ula be a goat with me and Pegeen?'

But Ula wanted to be the unicorn so it was decided. Midge told us that the unicorn was not allowed into the ark without a mate. He was told to pull the ark through the water by a rope tied to his horn. Brave and cheerful, the unicorn wasn't an animal of war.

So much was happening that Mamma didn't know about. Ula had a high soprano that had received notice. I was tone deaf and had periods, my fringe was curly. I was sick of worrying about my sisters. She'd had them, not me. While she sang to soldiers we'd be dancing in Noah's ark in darkness. We'd take the wind-up grammie into the chapel room. We'd play jolly tunes like 'Run Rabbit Run' and 'Roll out the barrel' and hoped the parents might like to sing. Red wanted 'In the Mood'. The animals wouldn't dance every minute, they'd need time for 'you-know-what'. As Mrs Noah, she would wear her black cotton skirt that her mum gave her, falling like petals round her calves. She would writhe and tangle with Noah in the darkness. Her skinny legs longed to be off.

There was no time to make costumes. We made botched attempts at finding ears and tails. The guests would proceed straight to the chapel room, having been welcomed by Ula at the gate. She hung paper chains round the stone unicorn's neck. I saw her kissing its ears.

The parents were used to watching interminable Bible scenes while the choir sang hymns year after year. Our show made a pleasant change. With our makeshift ears and tails you couldn't tell the difference between the Magnolias and the Clerkenwells who leapt and pranced before the dais. The sounds we made were mystifying to the parents, roaring, mooing, squeaking, barking; the caterwauling hurt the ears.

'Into the ark, you lot. In twos, please, you're bleeding soaked,' Red ordered.

In pairs we climbed up, welcomed by the Noahs. Ula was last, she stayed outside. Her cardboard horn was fixed by a rope round her head, she ran up and down pulling the ark. Noah held the other end. She was also in charge of the grammie, working the handle, making sure the tunes were jerky and fast. All we cared about was dancing, faster, faster. The parents started to smile. Nothing like a tune to relax and amuse you. What a quaint original show. Heels started tapping to the music, shoulders jiggled.

'Wind the grammie, you bloodclot.'

'I am. I'm trying to,' Ula answered. We were off again.

I looked in vain for Mamma, I knew it was hopeless. I saw Midge's parents and her father's dogcollar. The lights went off, we danced now in the dark. The parents' tapping and humming was less inhibited. One or two even took to the floor themselves, shuffling and swaying politely; it was after all just innocent fun. War entailed change, adjustment, classes mixed, standards slipped or disappeared. You did your best to pull with a will and keep cheerful. The music changed. It was 'In the Mood'. Mr and Mrs Noah circled each other. Mrs Noah advanced, lifting her skirts. She thrust her hips forward, put her arms up to Mr Noah, put her face and her thin lips to be kissed. The parents went quiet, someone coughed. I looked to the doorway. Was that Miss Gee in the passage wringing her hands? Her girls were unrecognizable, her pageant a mockery, we had desecrated her chapel room.

The finale came with my special tune that I'd asked Ula for, we would finish with a change of mood. 'When I grow too old to dream, Your love will live in my heart.'

The parents glowed with emotion. How lovely. Dreams never faded or palled. They stayed with you, you didn't outlive them, through wars and grey hairs dreams remained. I'm thinking of you, Mamma, I smell your perfume, this is your tune, why aren't you here? I'm thinking of the cakes and the couple kissing their ring, I'm thinking of your voice, your face, your smell.

'Bravo. Encore. More.'

We stepped down from the dais happily. Ula skipped round with her rope and horn. I was proud of her, proud of all of us. Bible Beasts was a great success.

Phoebe stretched her hand out, welcoming, explaining. Miss Gee was unwell. Yes, wasn't it a bore? Miss Patrice was nursing her, she and Red were in charge this evening. 'C'est la guerre,' she said, adding 'Vive la paix!' Red walked behind her, mincingly. 'That's right, poor old lady come over queer.' The girls done the show theirselves, glad you liked it. That old Bible stuff was old-fashioned, animals were more modern, made a change. Red fancied herself as good as a duchess, better than Phoebe, extending two fingers to touch each parent's hand. She invited them for a cup of tea. That's right, in the dining room. She ran the meals now, with a bit of help from old Phoeeb. She'd taught her how to cook, Phoeeb hadn't known nothing. She'd taught this school to dance as well. Pleased they liked it, come again next year. Cup of tea now, in the dining room, that's right. Red would make sure the whole evening went with a bang, they must leave with happy memories and bellies full.

I watched the fathers in uniform. If Papa hadn't died would he look like that? And would Mamma be by his shoulder smiling lovingly? Was it loneliness that kept her away? If she had him to love, would she love us better?

There was Phoebe's brother, more handsome than his photograph, the youngest and best-looking here. Phoebe touched his cheek with hers. 'At last, angel brother. I'd have been peeved if you hadn't come.'

He looked from her to me. He stared, I felt embarrassed. I had been so proud of my tail made of knotted stockings, the cardboard ears, the whiskers fashioned from string. I pulled at them. They felt silly. If only I had on my lovely blue dress.

'Bonnie, my brother wants to meet you. Come on, come on and be met.'

'How are you, Bonnie, under those whiskers?'

'I'm all right, thanks very much. Have you met Red?'

'I haven't yet. I intend meeting her. It's you I want to meet first. You make an adorable mouse, but I expect you know that?'

'No. Midge is a mouse too. Do you know her?'

'I know Midge. I'm interested in you. You looked so sweet and fervent during that last song. I'll bet you believe in dreams too. Do you?'

He spoke softly, as drawlingly as Phoebe. He took the hand that wasn't clutching my tail. Then he took that hand too, clasping them lightly, not letting them go. His fingers tingled, they felt exciting. He kept looking at me. Why did he want to meet me? Why did he want to know about dreams?

'I'm not sure. I suppose I do. I've ... I can't remember your name.'

'It's Percival. I loved the way you dance. You dance enchantingly. I longed to join you. Do you waltz? Will you waltz with me one day?'

'When? I'm not much good at the waltz. We never ...'

93

'Then I must teach you, mustn't I? You and I must waltz one day.'

Red's dancing was jerky and childish. I longed to be whirled across the floor with his arm round me while violins softly played. Outside would be a shining moon and roses smelling heavenly. But I was too shy to imagine being outside alone with him. It was safer to stay with the violins and candles, swirling and circling, our hair touching, our cheeks brushing, his pale eyes close to mine. When he smiled his cheeks flattened, he had Phoebe's bony jaw. Percival was a lovely name. He watched me as if I was special, something to be cherished. Sir Percival and the holy grail. It's you I want to meet. I longed to join you.

'You won't forget, Bonnie, will you? We will meet and we will waltz.'

'I'll never forget.' But when will it be? When?

I hadn't known my eyes were closed until I felt Red there, interrupting, spoiling the dream. Moonlight, roses, violins, candles, spoiled now, fading, gone. Go away, Red, you've spoiled everything. Get away, you Clerkenwell beast.

'You Perce? Thought you was. I'm Red, Phoebe's mate.'

Ed hadn't arrived, she hadn't given up hope, he still might turn up. Light Infantry. Christmas leave. She chewed her sandwich as she spoke, her short teeth biting quickly. That almost lipless mouth was used to kisses, she'd been trusted and loved by Ed. Percival watched with alert pale eyes. Light Infantry? Which detachment? Her boyfriend was a fortunate chap.

'And you, Bonnie. Have you someone special here tonight?'

'Mamma couldn't. There isn't . . .'

'Her dad is dead. Her mum didn't show up. Old Bonnie's been left in the lurch.'

'I'm not. I'm not.'

'Poor Bonnie. Never mind. You will remember your

94

promise to me, won't you?'

'What's she promising you, eh? Is Bonnie a dark horse after all? Cor . . . look who . . . Stone the crows, look at your teacher.'

In the dining-room doorway was the terrible figure of Miss Patrice. 'Come at once, someone. My sister . . . my sister . . .'

Phoebe showed leadership and strength. No time now for languor or affectation. Emergency stations, no confusion please. Her velvet heels tapped to the door. Miss Patrice? Well well, what is this. Let there be calm.

She helped her back to the rooms beyond the conservatory, leaving Red in charge. Midge only had authority out of doors. She didn't mind, she was leaving anyway, nor did she dislike Red whose ambitions differed from her own.

'Okay folks,' Red shouted. 'Keep your hair on. Stay as you were.'

She looked at Percival. Don't you move either, she'd be back in a tick, she'd just find out what was up.

Midge's father, experienced in pain and bewilderment, followed Phoebe and Red outside. He hadn't approved of the pageant, mildly blasphemous, an affront to the intelligence, but the two head girls were coping well. He suggested that we carry on with the supper while he saw what he could do.

We still wore our ears and tails and mixed up clothing. We went on handing out biscuits and tea.

'Afraid it's serious, folks. The old head teacher is dead.'

Red was there, licking her lips triumphantly. It was a thrill breaking such news. Ula gave a whimper like the noise she made in her nightmares. Her face looked awful. What did Red mean, 'dead'? Who was dead, explain it please, which person was it who had died? Tor put her arms round Ula, she stroked her hair, which earlier she had tried to plait like a unicorn's mane. Her hair straggled

95

from the rope with the horn tied to it. She was crying. Who could be dead?

'What I said, kiddo. Your head teacher snuffed it.' Serve her right, profiteering spiv.

I had to speak for Miss Gee and protect Ula. I said that the war had been too much for Miss Gee. Too many changes, she'd never wanted her school to be like this.

'You mean she didn't want us coming here from Clerkenwell. Well we didn't want to come.'

'I think Bible Beasts upset her. I think she saw us.'

'Everyone enjoyed theirselves, nothing wrong with it. We were doing the Bible.'

'The dancing might have shocked her, she's not used to it.'

'You don't know nothing about it, Bonnie.'

But Red was upset, I could tell. I felt Percival near me, touching my hand again. Then Midge's father returned. Yes, the news was true.

She had apparently died quite suddenly. The doctor had been sent for but hadn't arrived in time. In due course we would know the reason. It was sad and upsetting, a proof, if proof were needed, that our lives were not in our hands.

Red muttered something contemptuous. Midge's mother put down her cup. This, on top of the extraordinary exhibition the school had just put on, was proof of what they already suspected. The school wasn't suitable, the sooner they reclaimed Midge the better. She must start after Christmas elsewhere.

'I can't bear it. I don't know what you're talking about.' Ula clung to Tor, rubbing her eyes.

'Hush, darling. It will soon be over. There.'

Pegeen offered Ula a cough sweet. Barbie squeezed her hand.

I had never seen Ula look so white and unhappy. She had known so many deaths. She had liked Miss Gee and all the grace and elegance talk. The two sisters symbolized something we'd not experienced: certainty of purpose, principles and pride. I remembered that sad face behind the magnolia tree. Miss Gee had been proud of us once. Miss Patrice would never carry on without her. Though they'd disagreed, they had needed each other.

Midge's father went to the telephone again. He stood by the teapot. He had a suggestion to make. Those parents who could manage it might like to take their daughters home now. Leave at once without waiting for the end of term. Miss Patrice was in agreement, he saw no problem. Midge's mother asked about the London girls, what would happen to them? Phoebe drawled that Miss Patrice had suggested once that the Magnolias should invite the Clerkenwells home with them. There was silence. Phoebe winked at Red. Had she a secret plan perhaps, with Percival? The parents rustled uncomfortably; they murmured, trying to conceal their dismay. The jolly tunes and dancing earlier were forgotten, they began to wish they hadn't come. The London girls, though quaint and delightful, would scarcely be suitable guests in their homes. They lit cigars and cigarettes, they cleared their throats. It was war. To refuse would seem churlish and mean. Phoebe the head girl was unnecessarily masterful, urging and explaining as she moved from group to group. The girls had already been paired off for the pageant; stick to your animal partner, take that girl home if you could. She pushed her lank hair back, no need to fuss or delay. Just pack your things now and go. She told Ula kindly that Miss Gee had probably died without pain. Red copied Phoebe, pushing her frizzed hair back. Poor old person, snuffing it at Christmas. Rotten time to go. She'd not met her personally; she felt choked now it was too late. She was waiting for her boyfriend now. How about another cup of tea?

'Oh come on, Red. Percival wants . . .'

Red wasn't budging without her boyfriend. Ed would turn up, we'd see. Midge was pleading with her parents. Bonnie was her partner, let her come back, please. How I longed to sing carols in Midge's home and open presents; to help them cook their Christmas meal; to meet their pets and help care for them. Christmas with Midge would be a dream come true.

'But my sisters, Midge, I couldn't leave them. They'd never manage.' And there was my promise to Mamma.

'They could all come home, couldn't they, Mummy? All three of them. Say yes, please.'

The mother shook her head regretfully. Space was at a premium with their large family, especially at Christmas. One extra yes, three was too much.

'It's quite all right, Midge, don't feel badly. We'll be quite all right here on our own.'

I hated her worrying about me, I hated pity. She said she would give me all the mice if I liked.

'The whole cage? Are you sure?'

'Sure I'm sure.' And I must get in touch with my mother to tell her about Miss Gee dying. I didn't say I didn't know where to telephone. A cageful of mice would compensate for anything in life.

Her father must leave quickly because of the parish. It was better not to say goodbye. Midge had taught me everything I needed. Our friendship had been real, our times with the mice rapturous. I would miss her small eyes smiling and explaining. I would remember everything she'd told me, I would guard the cage with my life. I wished her farewell in silence. I will never forget you, Midge. Go forth, good friend and noble vet to be.

The dormitory was in an uproar. Parents had come up to help them pack. They were trying to behave hospitably, accepting their hostess role with grace. It was the giving time of year, the London children were neglected, poor little casualties. The ragged assortment of clothes was hard to believe. Where were the uniforms they'd so lovingly provided? Where were the soft underclothes, the expensive shoes? Barbie's mother held up a blouse with the sleeve torn out. A blazer had scraps of fur glued in place of the collar. Beds, floors, drawers were strewn with unwashed, unmended clothes. Beside the wash-basins was a communal pile of garments that no one wanted. Barbie's mother shook her head, she conferred with Midge's mother. Was this what they paid high fees for? Truly the cost of war was high, the sooner they left the better.

Red's vanilla smell was strong in the air, heightening the tension. Now that the Clerkenwells were leaving they were behaving as they had when they'd first come, silent, cold and hard. No one had asked them if they wanted to stay with these toffee-nosed parents. They were on their guard again. The days of sharing clothes, dancing and comics were coming to an end. There would be fresh criticism ahead. They didn't trust these Magnolia parents and their rich, unnatural ways. Grown-ups and teachers didn't change much, whether peace or war; you had to obey.

The Magnolias felt let down and embarrassed. Their friends were not presenting themselves in a good light. The world of school was already fading, the home world lay ahead. They bolstered their confidence with the old school slang, unused since the Clerkenwells came. They grinned and shoved each other. 'Same to you with brass knobs on', 'More than somewhat feeble', 'Catch me ere I swoon'. Basins were thumped back and forth for the last time. Curtains rattled, clothes were selected at random.

I bent over my pillow; I couldn't bear to lose Midge. She was leaving my life for ever, in a moment she'd be gone. I felt for my golden watch. I would give it to her as a memento; she'd admired it, her own was a cheap one. So much had happened since we'd stood in this dormitory and she'd told me her name. 'Midge is a mosquito,' I'd said. I looked up. Midge had left.

'Tough luck, kiddo. You're too late.' Red had seen.

They were all going. I sat on my bed with my sisters, listening and watching. 'Goodbye you three. Happy Christmas.' 'Bye-ze-bye.' 'Merry Chrissiewinks.' 'So long.'

There was just Red now, and us. She sat picking her nail polish, looking sulky. She'd shoot Ed when he turned up. Phoebe had left with that pale-eyed brother of hers; she never did trust a pale-eyed man. Perce was a typical la-di-da, unreliable. As for those profiteering spivs, the elder one was lucky to have kicked the bucket before the government caught her. She stood up, still in her black cotton skirt and someone's slippers. She'd go down again and wait for Ed.

'We'll sleep in the end beds, we might as well.' We'd become used to sleeping where we wanted, in the beds or sometimes on the floor.

Downstairs the dining room was heaped with empty plates. There was no tea left in the pot. The draining boards and kitchen table were covered with used cutlery and crumbs. We licked our fingers and pressed them to the crumbs as we used to at home. What was Miss Patrice doing? Had the ambulance born the body to the mortuary? Was Miss Gee praying with the angels now? If only Ula would stop using her hair for a hanky. She looked so frightened. These deaths were spoiling our lives.

We went to bed without undressing or washing. Red's vanilla and stale powder-puff smell had got in my brain. I would lie still and think about Percival, I would think of roses, moonlight, violins. I would remember his hands touching, his voice speaking, I would remember him for the rest of my life. I would keep my promise, I would waltz with him one day.

I heard the sound of the front door bell and then the sound of slippered feet.

'Halt who goes there?' Ula cried in a dramatic way.

'Shut your face, it's only me.'

Red was close to me, smelling of something different, like sherry, but sharper and thick. Her whispering was thick against my ear, her thin lips like little worms wet and tickling.

'We're stopping in the other dorm. Don't tell your sisters.'

'You mustn't, Red. You shouldn't. Don't.'

'You're just jealous, you little bloodclot. We don't want any spinsters spoiling it.'

She wouldn't have dared if Phoebe had been here. This was a school for girls. She shouldn't bring Ed up. And I wasn't a spinster, I was a prefect. As a matter of fact, I could be head girl now. I closed my eyes and tried to forget her. Think of Percival again. Think of waltzing and feeling him touch you. Feel his hands, feel his flat cheek against yours. Pale lips, pale eyes extracting promises, waltzing, dreaming in moonlight all our lives.

Tor shook me. 'There's a noise in the other dorm. What is it? Wake up, Bonnie, there it is again.'

'Don't listen, it's imagination. I was having a dream.'

Ula woke. 'What is it? Who goes there?'

There was something, Tor repeated. A horrid noise. There it was again. We must find out, it was our duty; it might be Germans. Or burglars, Ula added, or poisoned gas. Her gas mask was ready, just in case.

I went first. Our bare feet were soundless. Past the swing basins rimmed with dirt. We passed the cupboards, empty now and the musty bath cubicles. Someone in the other dorm was in dreadful pain.

We stood in the doorway. I didn't want to look. I had to look. I felt sick and hot and cold. I must stop my sisters looking. It was a noise like animals. Go away, Red, it's not allowed.

There were four, two on the floor under a blanket, two

on the bed by the door. The light shone on Percival and Red, they had no clothes on. Their bodies were spread, she was on top of him, her bottom jerked up and down. They rolled, he was above her, heaving and pushing. Panting, awful, they weren't wearing clothes. They seemed joined below the waist, they must separate, we must stop watching. I couldn't stop, I was excited. Why didn't they stop? They didn't want to stop, they liked it, it wasn't pain, the noises were noises of love.

The two under the blanket were wriggling and squirming.

'I'll teach you, like I done Red. Stuck up bitch, leave it to me, I'll teach you.'

And Phoebe, our head girl, our goddess, 'Don't hurt. Don't stop. Stop. More. Oh put out the flags.'

We didn't speak or look at each other. We got into our beds again.

# TEN

Everything was worse when you were tired. My brain was overcharged. My sisters and I might have been mistaken. Could they have been practising some kind of dance? Why had Percival been there? Why did Phoebe say she wanted more?

It hadn't been dancing, it had been sexual intercourse.

Phoebe was nearly sixteen, Red was thirteen. Was it legal? Could you do it if you had no bust? Red had no hair below either, she didn't have periods, but her spitty lips were used to kissing and being kissed. I knew about babies now, thanks to Midge. A man put his dangling thing between your legs and put juice there. Red called that part her naughty-naughty. Could she have the ingredients of a child in her? Midge hadn't told me about noises or heaving. I had never seen a dangling thing, except for Bruno's, under the Christmas tree, before he died. I had imagined that both people would have to keep quite still as it went in, barely breathing and keeping straight legs. Now I saw why it had to be done in bed or under covers. It was so noisy and so rude.

The whole thing was Red's fault, I'd never forgive her. But for Red, Phoebe would be safely asleep in a room next to Percival at the Black Lion Hotel. I never wanted to set eyes on her, rude Clerkenwell beast. She had spat on the hospitality of our school, had disgraced the memory of Miss Gee. The whispering behind curtains with Red had been the start of Phoebe's downfall, her mind had been poisoned. Clerkenwell people were different, the children grew up quickly. It wasn't necessary to do sexual intercourse until you were married and wanted babies. Red was tainted. If only Midge were here.

A car drove out of the drive very early. Did Phoebe know we had seen? We heard sniggering and splashing in the bathroom. Red came to collect her clothes.

'Don't go in there yet, spinster.'

She was disgusting, I'd never use that bath again. Could a dangler go into you in a bath, did it work under water too? Midge said that nature was beautiful and miraculous; she might not think that now. They had used Magnolia House for disgusting purposes, without asking. They hadn't even paid. Ed, who had sealed his picture with a kiss for Red, had never met Phoebe. What could Percival have seen in Red? She'd called him snotty-nosed, la-di-da and treacherous, why had she changed?

Percival had held my hands and made them fluttery. I rubbed them now on my sheet. They felt as if they'd been bitten. I wasn't a spinster, I was my sisters' elder sister.

'What's up? Cat got your tongue?'

I wouldn't answer. Let her do anything she wanted as long as I didn't know.

'Red, wait. What about breakfast? Who will make it?'

Trust Ula to think about food. Red called back to make it herself. 'I ain't stopping here with you lot. Murderers.'

We were silent. What had she meant?

I will put Red out of my mind for ever. I will forget that Clerkenwell exists. The fire-fighting dad and his beer on Saturday, that mum making bangers and stew, the shiny coal scuttle, the dog warming its fur by the fire, are all contaminated. I will never again think about Ed. The four of them had lost their reason. People had mental black-outs in wartime, they got shell-shocked and did strange things. Nothing mattered if my sisters were safe. I haven't changed, I'm the same, my sisters' protectress and friend. I will look after them this Christmas, make it up to them. Happiness shouldn't have to be earned. Midge thought that all knowledge was important and useful. I wish we hadn't been there last night. Phoebe of the sophistication and elegance will join the army. Her boredom and string-coloured beauty won't fail her. I don't think she'll ever have inner grace. Pale-haired Percival, knight in armour, did you really want to waltz with me?

Tor stroked my hands. 'I'm here. Don't look like that. It's not your fault that everything is suddenly horrible.'

'Tor, I want to show you something that Midge and I did. You mustn't tell anyone, not even Ula. I'm going to need you to help.'

'It's in the garden. I know about the incinerator. And about periods.'

'I hoped you didn't. You're too young.'

Anything to do with bodily development, sexual inter-course or death was better left unknown as long as poss-ible. Tor believed that if you learned things early they didn't frighten you. It was your own brain that made things bad.

'You'll like the surprise. It's small and wonderful.'

'Will I?'

'Oh yes.'

I would teach her to tear up nest wool and handle the babies. With time and effort we might even teach them tricks.

While Ula made the breakfast Tor and I went down the path. We were close again, it was like the old days, before school, before meeting Midge. Tor had been left out. We were reunited. I would always love her more than anyone, because I knew her so well. We might even become world famous mouse experts.

We passed the allotments, ready for the spring planting of vegetables. The school had no staff left. When we went, there would be no girls.

There had been another hard frost. We breathed like dragons to make smoke come. On the path was one of the croquet hoops, forgotten from the lawn. I kicked it, chunks of frost fell off. I thought of our first night here. We had kicked the hoops and Ula pretended to be trapped and we had expected to be here for the rest of the war. I must write to Mamma today.

'Remember the sun in Ireland, Tor. The war spoiled everything. Oh hurry up, do.'

She said things might have changed in any case, because of getting older. She wanted to say something, must I go so fast?

I couldn't wait to get there. I wanted to see her face. Past the incinerator smelling sickly, past the rubbish dump and potting sheds as tidy as little homes now, thanks to Midge and I.

'Wait, Bonnie, I want to tell you ...'

'Shut your eyes now, Tor. Breathe in. Smell. Can you guess? *Tor*. Oh Tor. Look.'

I couldn't stop screaming, I couldn't stop shouting. Someone had opened our cage. The mice had escaped, they had been murdered. There were traps in a row on the floor. In each trap was a bloodied mouse. There was the black one with its eyes bulging, dried blood on its snouty nose. There was the sweet piebald with its neck broken, there was the mother stiff and cold. There was one pale tail apart from the mousetraps, its pink root tipped with blood.

'They've been killed, they've been murdered. They're gone, Tor.'

She was shaking too, her cheeks were wet, tears dripped

106

and splashed from her face. 'Oh the poor things, look at them, oh the poor things.'

'I'll write to Mamma. Blow your nose.' I had never seen her crying properly before.

'I haven't ... Oh Bonnie, what shall we do?'

'Use mine. Who could have done it? Who could be so wickedly cruel?'

'We'll have to bury them, we can't just leave them. We mustn't let Ula find out.'

'She hates blood. We must do it now. We'd better find a spade.'

We parcelled each corpse in twists of newspaper. There was no proper prayer we could say. 'Run in peace,' we whispered, folding each packet. We would bury them outside the hut. We must leave here now, it wasn't suitable for children. I wouldn't wait to tell Mamma. We took it in turns with the spade, trying to dig, pushing and kicking it. We could barely dent the frost-covered ground.

'Listen, there's Ula calling. She mustn't see.'

I ran to the potting sheds to call to her. We're coming, don't come out in the cold, we're coming.

'We can't bury them, Bonnie, it's too hard. What shall we do?'

We flung the bundles into the incinerator. Don't think about it, think of your sisters, just throw them away and run. This is worse than Miss Gee dying or Bruno, worse than the orgy in the dormitory, it's the saddest thing of my life.

'Listen to me, both of you. We're leaving here. At once.'

'Why, Bonnie? We must have breakfast. I've made it. What were you both doing so long?'

'We were just tidying. What did you make?'

'Tea and bread. I found some raspberry jam.'

No wonder Tor was small and scrawny and Ula had spots on her chin. We hadn't eaten properly since we got here. We'd had no lessons and no clean clothes.

107

'There's a letter from Mamma, Bonnie.'

'Darlings, I hope your Christmas at the school will be jolly. Isn't it a shame the army commandeered our home? I'm staying at the White Harte Hotel at present. I may have news for you all soon. The company travels north after Christmas. I think of you and miss you.'

'Going north? Where in the north?' We must leave at once, we must see her.

There was no answer when I knocked at Miss Patrice's door. She was sitting at Miss Gee's desk like a statue. Her head was down, she stared at the blotting paper pad, her hands lay upwards on the desk. Her hair was dry and neglected.

'So you see, Miss Patrice, we can't stay. There's no one to look after us. We've decided to go home. If you'll just lend us our fares.'

She didn't look up or answer me. I took two pounds from her box on the windowsill. 'Save for the brave.'

Was she fit to be left? Was it safe? 'I'm sorry for the trouble,' I murmured. My sisters came first.

'We mustn't forget our gas masks.' Ula was excited, getting her case out, trying to whistle again. There was nothing much left to pack. We found three old coats from the communal pile, with rips in them. The word 'uniform' had lost its charm. I would never wear any again if I could help it. I felt for my watch. I'd so wanted Midge to have it. I had so much to remember her by. She had nothing of me. My watch was gone. There was a note. 'Midge told Pheeb about you and your sisters how Ula killed that girl and you and Tor letting your brother catch his death. You needn't give yourself such airs I seen those dead mice too Tor done it. So long Ethelreda.'

Ethelreda? It was from Red. So Midge had told Phoebe about our family secrets, Phoebe had told Red. Did the whole school know? I could trust no one, they were all traitors. It didn't matter now. Tor would never do anything cruel, I wouldn't believe that. It had probably been Gumm who had trapped the mice, or even Red herself.

I longed for my scruffy home clothes again, my old-fashioned bodice, my jerseys. The magic of disorder and muddle was over. Everything here was a bad dream. Miss Patrice had smelled of mould, we smelled nasty ourselves.

We had learned little of importance here that would help in the outside world. We could write copperplate and dance and make tea. I had failed in the keeping of mice. I hadn't even buried them. They lay in filth in the incinerator with half-burned sanitary towels. I had rolled that single bloodied tail in my pink hankie. Run in peace.

The taxi drove us past the unicorn. We saw his face for the last time. I didn't look back. He was just something made of stone, no protection against betrayal and death. No wonder the cheeseplant was dying in the conservatory. The whole place was as good as dead.

Now we are back at our own station, the platform is empty, the waiting room is locked. No stationmaster or porter to smile and take our tickets. Have they too been called to fight? The little side gate is open, we are on the road now. We will walk up the hill to our town.

'Here's the White Harte. Perhaps Mamma is in there. I can't see anyone.'

Ula craned her neck to the windows with their old-fashioned leaded panes. She started pushing the front door. We must ring for attention at the reception desk; she'd been in Irish hotels, was used to them.

'Don't start showing off again, Ula. We'll go home. Mamma might be there.'

I didn't want them to know that I was afraid of hotels. I wanted home as much as I wanted Mamma. It might be bombed or altered, our things might have disappeared. My head felt light and dizzy as if nothing was really true. Could this be happening? Had we really run away from school? And did Mamma realize that Ula was a sort of murderer and that Tor and I were almost as bad? Bruno had seemed sweet without his clothes, we'd meant no harm, nor had Ula. Red saw us as criminals, three guilty sisters with blood on our hands. I couldn't blame Mamma for wanting to be a film star or a singer, she was probably ashamed of us. We were three killer daughters who got on her nerves.

Soon her rose-smelling kisses and orange curls would cast their spell again. We would see her and start to adore her. She should have warned me about periods and inter-course, we should have known more about death. Midge was right, worries increase if you don't discuss them. I must find out more about Ula in Ireland, I need to talk about Bruno's death. I don't think Tor is well – all that sweating. When we find Mamma we must talk.

Lorries filled with soldiers kept overtaking us, convoys were passing through our town. Soldiers in waterproof trousers and tin helmets rode on motor bikes. An officer in a mud-coloured car swished past, the tyres making crunchings in the frost. Our gas masks and cases felt heavy now. I wanted a cup of school tea.

'Fancy a ride? Jump up, kiddo.'

'Don't smile at him, Ula. We don't know him. Do hurry, we're nearly there.' Perhaps the soldier was from London. Red said 'kiddo'. Don't smile.

And then we were home again. Changed-looking, cold, unfriendly, under frost-covered tiles. Our curtains were gone, our front door was open. Where had our hall carpet gone?

Was it to save it from soldiers' dirty boots? Why was the standard lamp missing and the coat rack? Where was the letter tray and the umbrella stand? What was the funny smell?

Through the open school-room door we could see a filing cabinet and the corner of a table. Someone was using a typewriter. The sound of plates clattering came from the basement. We were hungry and thirsty, we wanted dinner. A drawer slammed shut in the school room, boots sounded on the boards.

'Hey up. This is army premises. You're on army property here. No kiddies, no civilians, what's up then? Eh lass, no need for tears.'

He looked down at the manilla envelopes he was holding, avoiding my face until I felt better. I blinked.

'Just ... we wondered if Mamma was here. It's our home, we used to live here. Mamma is at the White Harte, but ...'

'No babies, no kiddies, no mammas. Who is she? She did live here?'

'It's our house, I told you. Mamma is an actress, well she's a singer now really. We must find her, she's going north, you see.'

He shuffled his envelopes. Steady now, calm down, girl. Nothing was worth being that upset. He shouted down the basement stairs.

'Illingworth, come up here will you? Some kiddies are asking for their mam. She sings, she's a singer seemingly, used to live here. Happen we can help, eh? You'd better come.'

# ELEVEN

Illingworth's army plimsolls seemed almost as long as his shinbones. A dishcloth hung from his khaki apron. He threw another cloth like a ball from hand to hand.

'Oh hullo, do you live here too now?'

In spite of Ula's troubles she was never frightened of strangers. Her lock of hair stuck up questioningly, as if she'd whitened it with frost.

The men's faces both looked well lived-in, with wrinkled skin round their eyes, but they weren't old. They looked at you straight when they spoke to you, they had flat accents and came from the north. I knew they were kind from the way they looked at me. They had hard, scraped-looking jaws. I'd never spoken to a soldier apart from Percival. Was it for these men that Mamma sang?

Singing was more elegant than dancing. I wouldn't like her kicking up her knickers in front of men. Would she sing special songs for Christmas? How I wished we had gone to Midge's family to sing round her tree with her pets.

Our school room was called the orderly room now. The soldier in charge was Oxenbury. Both spoke with shortened vowels and called us lass a lot.

'Our piano has gone,' Ula said, coming from our drawing room across the hallway. The men ate there, sitting at
long tables with folding legs and wooden fold-up chairs.
Our lesson table with the chenille cloth in our school room
was replaced by Oxenbury's desk and files. He had wire
baskets for his letters, labelled 'In', 'Pending', and 'Out'.
He had a modern telephone that you held in one hand,
instead of our old one with the separate ear-piece that you
hung on a hook at the side.

His typewriter was called the 'Good Companion' and
was kept under a cloth cover. He was dapper, with short
scrubbed nails and hands. His trouser creases were like
knife blades, the tucks in his battle dress were pressed like
fans. Illingworth moved swiftly in his light soles. The
kitchen work was heavy, all food must be carried upstairs.
The hair over both their collars was so short that their
necks looked shaved. The curls grew strongly over their
crowns. With their odd speech and their thick eyebrows
they might have been brothers. They were best mates and
they liked us, you could tell. Oxenbury was the gentle
one. Illingworth spoke less but didn't mince his words.
Children were not allowed but we made a diversion. The
rest of the section were out on manoeuvres on this frosty
afternoon.

'Happen you fancy tea then?'

'Yes please, Illingworth. Just what I wanted. Can I help
you?'

'Ula, we don't live here now. Don't be cheeky.'

Ula was letting the family down as usual, strutting
about with her toes turned out, touching their telephone,
poking at the Good Companion. Now she had the cheek
to want to serve tea. We didn't know these men.

We sat at Oxenbury's desk feeling better. The newly
painted hot pipes smelled like lentil soup. Our home
looked more sombre now, the army furnishings were
plain. They had had problems, Illingworth said, with the

heating system; army maintenance had soon put it right.

'Do you like our house?'

'Not a lot to complain of, better than some billets I've seen. We got rid of the dry rot. Did you know you had dry rot, back of the pantry sink?'

'What is dry rot? I've never heard of it, Illingworth.'

Ula fiddled her fingers into the mesh of the In tray. If only she would keep still. Illingworth said you paid dear for neglect of property, but my family would stand to gain in the long run, thanks to the army who let nothing go to rack. He was a regular soldier, he'd moved around a lot. Not like Oxenbury here, in for the present emergency. Come peace, Oxenbury would be off home again.

'Tor and I never went to the basement very much. Ula did. We never knew about the dry rot.'

I wondered if humans could catch it. Perhaps Mamma had dry rot of the heart. I wanted to defend our home and family from criticism. They should realize that our father was dead, that Mamma had done wonders, that but for this war we'd be living here now. I asked Oxenbury what he had done before he joined up, if he'd always lived in the north? He took a comb from his pocket to repart his curls. He had worked in a wholesale drapery business in Scarborough, had been in charge of stock control. Army life suited him. He'd like to be a quartermaster, that was his dream. He liked order, liked things done right. He flicked his Good Companion with his handkerchief. Aye, army life suited him champion. Not but what he'd be back to civvy street when time came, choose how.

'There'll be changes. Old life won't be the same. War was bound to happen. Change for the best.'

'What do you mean, Illingworth? What kind of change?'

Illingworth spoke of class struggle, of social change that would affect one and all. Servants had gone already, good luck to them. So-called gentry must do their own chores. Stately mansions would be a thing of the past come peace-

time, turned into museums or blocks of flats. Upper classes took too much for granted, working man must have
his chance. Too much was owned by too few people,
present capitalism was due to die. He wasn't like
Oxenbury, he believed in red politics.

'They're kiddies, Illingworth, don't confuse them.
You're too quick to start waving the red flag.'

'I quite understand, thanks very much. What I want to
know is where are our things?'

Capitalists, dry rot, flags and changes, what we needed
was our old home clothes. Once I had my skirt and jersey,
my brain might begin to feel real. I was wearing Pegeen's
vest under this awful overcoat. Ula had the blazer with the
glued-on fur. Oxenbury told us that everything in the
place was army issue. Any inquiries regarding previous
effects should be addressed to War Office.

'We had a brother once. Our nursery was on the top
floor. But he's dead now, he died last Christmas.'

'*Ula*. Shut up, can't you?'

She was without dignity or shame, blurting out our
private affairs to strangers. I was sick of her. Before Tor
and I had left Ireland we'd planted a magic stone to draw
us back there. If only we could be there now.

'Eh lass, she meant no harm. Don't get yourself upset
again.'

'I'm not upset. I was just thinking about Ireland. We
stayed there before the war.'

Oxenbury had a sister living there himself. He said
everything ended some time, both good and bad, else
how would there be change? Folk often only realized a
good experience when it was over. He spoke so kindly, I
longed to confide. I wanted to explain about my sisters
and how I wanted a rest from them. I wished they were
like other children, who hadn't had deaths to put up with,
who hadn't lived so much on their own. Ula was eyeing
the soldiers' gas masks as if they were diamonds. They

had webbing straps and long breathing tubes hanging from large face-pieces.

'Fancy a biscuit?'

Oxenbury kept chocolate ones in his desk drawer for hungry moments during his important office work.

'Yes please. I'm quite hungry. I'll just look upstairs first, just in case, if I may?'

'Ula, Mamma isn't here. You know she isn't.'

Oxenbury said let her look to satisfy herself. But make haste before the section returned. She'd find all changed upstairs any road.

'Oh, all right then. Hurry, Ula.'

What had Illingworth meant about homes being turned into flats? Wouldn't we come back to live here? I would hate to be like the Clerkenwells eating chips and playing in the slums.

'Cheer up, lass. Look on the sunny side.'

The biscuits were digestive with chocolate on one side. They made a chocolaty burst when you bit. A luxury not often seen in shops now, he said. Tor ate slowly, Illingworth dipped his into tea, Oxenbury made polite little rattlings in his throat when he swallowed. We shared the serviceable army spoon.

'Chocolate biscuits, my favourite,' Ula said, coming down again from checking upstairs. From her face I knew she had seen something peculiar.

'What did you find, Ula?'

'Our eiderdowns and beds have gone.'

'Are there curtains?' Or did the soldiers have to dress and undress themselves in the dark? The orderly room windows were criss-crossed with brown paper to stop glass shattering in an air raid. Outside in the garden where our lavender used to grow were sandbags piled like a little wall. Ula said that their beds were miserable. Their mattresses split into three sections that they stacked in a pile during the day. Illingworth said they called them 'biscuits'. The rooms smelled of Jeyes fluid and everything was painted brown. I knew Ula had seen something that had upset her.

'Did you look in the nursery? Well, did you?'

'Captain's room is at the top now,' Oxenbury said. And he'd be in right trouble if it were known he'd let strangers in there. He glanced at Illingworth. The lass should have stayed below with us.

'Ula, what was it?'

Just an ordinary bed, she said, with a mattress and bedspread. There was a bedside table and proper curtains and ...

'What, Ula? And what?'

'Happen you saw a picture, lass? Yes?'

'What picture? Who of?'

She twisted her fingers. She'd seen Mamma's photograph. Taken long ago, with us when we were young.

'How could it be us? No one knows us here now.'

Could Mamma have given the captain a souvenir because she was going north? Film stars gave photographs to fans. I didn't want anyone looking at us here. Our house was all brown paint and change now, we didn't belong. Nothing felt real.

Oxenbury said slowly that a picture was nothing to get worked up about. Our mam was a singer, he'd seen her himself, they both had. The three of us should feel right proud. He smiled at us with his kind dog's smile. He didn't understand how much we missed her or how much she had let us down. In his part of the world mothers were probably different, more like Clerkenwell ones. They made nice dinners and put the children first. If they worked it would be for the children, not to amuse themselves. These men probably wrote home each week and got letters back. Was it possible that the picture was an advertisement for Mamma's show? The lovely singer with

118

her children at home. I was proud of our lovely mother. Oxenbury didn't understand. I was angry with her, I hated her. She never gave a photograph to me. It was Christmas, where was she now? Did she have her arms round us? What clothes did we have on?

I explained that she had wanted to be a film star, she was a singer now instead. It was her war work. Illingworth said in a dry voice that neglecting kiddies might not seem so patriotic to some. Not just term but holidays too. Some might not understand that. Did anyone know we were here?

'It's the bombs, you see,' Ula explained.

That was why Mamma wasn't here. She wanted us to be safe. She couldn't be expected to know the headmistress would die.

Tor said nothing. She'd been wonderful about the mouse slaughtering. In an emergency she didn't fail. Nothing would ever make me believe that she'd hurt them, she was loyal. I wished she could be more like Ula and Ula more like her.

'Magnolia House is a small school with a lovely uniform. Mamma bought it herself, it cost a lot.'

I looked down at our awful clothes. No one must think ill of Mamma. Ula started rustling in the drawer for another biscuit. 'And please excuse my little sister. She's had a tiring day.'

'Aye it would seem so. Don't you worry girl. Captain is a good bloke.'

'As I said Mamma is a singer. Actually she's a ... *chanteuse*.'

A rose-scented *chanteuse* of distinction waiting for us to join her.

'We know. We heard. We saw her. Listen up, that's Captain now.'

A car drew up, heavy feet sounded, lighter ones followed. Steps crossed the hall to the orderly room. A man

119

is in the doorway, Mamma is behind him. She is here, Mamma has come.

'Bonnie? What's this, what are you doing? You naughty ... why are you here?'

I had never seen her look so red and furious. She was trying to smile, she had little lines round her eyes. Her face was like a cracked dish. Why had we disobeyed her? She'd made arrangements for us. I was a naughty, disobedient girl.

'We couldn't stay. Miss Gee died. We had to leave, so we came.'

'Dead? She can't be dead. I saw her. When?'

Mamma had said she'd miss us and think of us. She had this captain now by her side. We were a nuisance, we had turned up unexpectedly, we were just a nasty surprise. The captain was the man we'd seen earlier in his shiny mud-coloured car. His face was like a ferret, staring now at Mamma.

She tried to settle her expression, smiling harder, twitching her shoulders. The captain mustn't see her looking upset. She spoke in a silly way, as gushingly as the Magnolias when they'd arrived at school.

'These are my three pets, aren't they sweet?'

'Mamma ... I ... I ...'

'Don't mumble, darling child. Bad manners. Now then, we must make a plan.'

'What kind of plan? We're here.'

'A plan for where you should go. Oh my god, Bonnie, what *have* you got on? Look at you.'

My vest, Ula's glue-furred blazer and Tor's blouse were a show. She was ashamed of us as well as vexed. We had interrupted her life, what must the captain think? Oxenbury and Illingworth had shown more welcome.

Ula spoke. 'What Bonnie meant was that school turned out horrible so we came back to you. I can sing now, Mamma, and I can read.'

'*Marvellous*, darling.'

'At our pageant I was a unicorn. I was alone. Where shall we go now?'

'Let me think, my sweet. A plan, we must make a plan. Let me think.'

'Hurry and think, please, Mamma. Bonnie is upset. We came by train.'

Ula was speaking her mind bravely, defending us without thought for herself. I wanted to hug her.

Mamma touched her bright curls. She gazed at the captain. Such a dilemma, what should she do?

Lorries were coming to a halt outside. Soldiers were shouting, manoeuvres were over. They would stamp across our hallway and up to our bedrooms, they would wash in our basins, blow smoke out of our windows, eat supper in our drawing room, having read the letters sorted by Oxenbury. The ferret-faced captain would go to the nursery to look at Mamma's picture. Would he sing while he shaved his face in the nursery bathroom? Would he plant a kiss on her face before he slept? His hair was short like the men's hair, he had blue stubble over his neck and chin. His nose jutted over his long shaped mouth. It wasn't that he was ugly that made him unlikeable, it was the way he looked at Mamma.

'What *shall* we do? I'm at a loss.'

'Do? I fail to see a problem. They must simply go to the hotel.'

'But ...'

'No buts. I shall see to it. I shall take you. The four of you shall come with me now.'

He looked better when he smiled, his eyes went kinder, but not as kind as Oxenbury, not the smile of a proper friend.

'And drive in an army car?' Ula squealed with pleasure. Could she sit in front?

We were a proud party, walking past the soldiers and

the lorries; we were the captain's guests. A weak sun was coming through the fog now and it didn't seem as cold. We would be spending Christmas with our Mamma. We would stay at the White Harte Hotel.

'Really, darlings, those *clothes*. What have you been up to? Where is your luggage?'

I explained that we'd just brought our washing things. Where were our old home clothes? She closed her eyes exhaustedly, she leaned her head back against the seat. So many decisions, so many problems. It seemed the army had requisitioned her life as well as her home. Her poor lambs were destitute and travel-stained, they had scarcely a stitch to wear.

'We couldn't bring anything. Miss Gee died, I told you. And everything went wrong.'

She said we looked pale. We seemed larger. Had we got taller?

'Ula has. I might have. But not Tor, she never grows. I ... Mamma, I'm older ... I ...'

'I know my sweet. I can see you are. Tell me later all about that.'

Her eyes looked at me, she didn't see me. She was thinking about the captain in front.

Then we were at the White Harte again, with the wisteria branches round the leaded windows. In the summer its flowers would be mauve. We were to share a large room overlooking the road.

'I can see the lorries passing.'

Ula would take the single bed by the window. Tor and I would share.

'Couldn't I share with you two, Bonnie? Why is it always you and Tor?'

'It isn't. Not always,' Tor said quietly. Ula should be allowed to join us sometimes, it wasn't kind or fair to keep her out.

# TWELVE

'Did you hear Mamma come in last night, Tor? Did she say goodnight?'

I had tried to stay awake, I had listened to the convoys of lorries passing and wondered if all those soldiers would get blown to bits. This must be the troop movements that Miss Gee spoke of. Our careless talk could cost their lives.

Our room was beautiful, we had loved it immediately. We had our own bathroom in the passage outside. Our clothes cupboard was like a separate room that you could walk in, with rails and shelves inside. We had hung up our raggy coats and explored our bathroom. We had arranged our toothbrushes and sponges on the shelves. We had brushed our hair and watched our reflections. Ula tapped her toothbrush on various surfaces to make different notes. Glass made the highest ones. Tor and I smiled tolerantly at her. We were three sisters come to rest at last in a hotel. We smeared our faces with Mamma's cold cream again. We lay in hot water to our ear lobes, forgetting about saving for the brave. Freedom was the White Harte Hotel, doing what we wanted, knowing that Mamma was near. In deep water you could forget growing older and being responsible, your brain and your feelings worked as one. Magnolia House was a distant nightmare, Mamma's room was on the same floor. She would look in to say goodnight after her show. Had she brushed kisses on our sleeping foreheads? I sniffed my hair for the scent of roses. 'Ula, did you hear Mamma?'

'I was watching for lorries. I was awake ages. I heard the people leaving the bar downstairs.'

She looked pink and normal again but Tor still looked sickly. The road was quiet. It was foggy again. The fog came in swirls, the sounds outside were muffled, once or twice a plane passed overhead. Runnels of wet ran down the little windows. Ula had put 'U's in each pane. It was early still, Ula wanted to go to the bathroom again, excitement made her like that. Mamma's bedroom faced the back.

I had a bedside lamp with a switch hanging from a length of silkbound flex. I felt it and remembered the mouse tail. Tor was rooting in her attaché case on the floor.

'Are you looking for your diary? Listen, Tor, I want to tell you something.'

'What are you saying, Bonnie? You always have secrets. You're leaving me out again.'

'Nothing, Ula. Watch for lorries or something.'

'Tell me. *Tell* me.'

'Don't keep her out, Bonnie. Tell.'

'Oh all right. I was asking Tor if she remembered our game.'

It was more a phantasy than a game which she and I had played for years. Once at Magnolia House I'd forgotten it, there had been neither privacy nor time. We used to make lairs in our beds and pretend to be animals. You could play it alone but it was better with Tor. We could pull our beds together to make a smooth base for a cave or nest. We made our eiderdowns and sheets into passages, propping the roof with a coat hanger or even a chair.

Wriggling and snuffling we became hedgehogs or badgers, moles or squirrels; we preferred burrowing animals rather than fierce ones, though Tor used to choose yaks or camels sometimes for a change. Then we'd drape clothes over cupboards and tables. Our game had no beginning and no end, our time was mostly spent in preparing the hide-outs. Tucking and smoothing and hoisting was a pleasure. This large hotel bed would be ideal. I didn't want Ula playing and spoiling it. I explained that it wasn't a proper game, she wouldn't enjoy it. Look for lorries and leave us alone.

'There aren't any. Please, Bonnie.'

Her cheek had a red mark from the crease of her pillow, her white lock of hair was on end.

'Let her, Bonnie, don't push her out.'

'Oh well. Think of an animal. Make a nest.'

'I'm a fly. Buzz buzz.'

'A fly isn't an animal, you fool. It's an insect.'

'I'll be a stone unicorn then.'

'If it's stone it can't make a nest, stupid. Play properly or you can't play at all.'

'I was the unicorn in the pageant.'

'Remember what Midge said about unicorns, Bonnie? They did exist once.'

The game was my invention. I didn't want Tor making the rules. Ula made me feel ashamed. She was fiddling with her pencil in her curls, trying to make another horn. She was so babyish and eager. I wanted to forget school and that unicorn on the gate and the pageant.

'Bonnie, why don't you be a mother unicorn? Then Tor and I can be your young.'

'I'm not being anyone's mother, thanks very much. And put that pencil down.'

'Let her, Bonnie, it won't hurt us.'

'They aren't real. No one ever saw one. It's stupid.'

My feeling of not existing was starting. Think of who

you are and why you're here. Christmas is coming, nothing is terrible, you needn't feel afraid any more.

'Oh all right.'

Ula thought that unicorns might sleep in grassy glades with ferns for covering. In summer they might lie on a lawn. We walked round quietly on hands and feet, shaking imaginary horns. Ula pawed the air looking solemn; she made little humming sounds. Being fond of moonlight it was probable that they sang at night. They would eat rose petals with jam, and a little fruit in the summer months. Unicorns were loving animals who didn't quarrel or fight. It was calming to roam round our room, being neither male nor female, adult nor child, just three sisters in accord. We played until we were tired of it, then we lay on the floor under our beds.

'Let's remember Ireland.'

The lovely warm summer seemed like years ago when we'd run and rolled on the grass. We had searched for four-leafed clovers and picked daisies, breathing that special summer smell. We had listened to bats squeaking and unseen dark night birds. We had run races in the twilight, never caring who won or lost. We were without past or future, only the present mattered. The war came and we'd had to come home. Why should good things have to end?

'The captain is Irish,' Ula sucked her hair.

'He isn't. Is he, Tor?'

'Ula was there the longest. He might be. Ula should know.'

'I don't trust him.'

Tor said he was kind to get us here, he'd been responsible. Mamma liked him.

'You don't think ...?'

Mamma wouldn't do anything stupid would she? We were used to not having men by now, a stepfather would be a burden. We didn't need one so why should she? Just because she wriggled and blinked at him didn't make him special.

'Mamma likes being looked after and protected. He's kind. She's been alone for so long.'

I said I didn't see why, she'd got us, hadn't she? Tor had a way of tucking her chin in when she was being sensible. She was too wise and old-fashioned for her age. She understood grown-ups and children better than I did. I was too old now for playing games on the floor but I'd enjoyed it. After what had happened to Ula you'd think she'd never want to see an Irish person.

'Feel, Bonnie, feel my horn.'

'Shut up, don't be so stupid. I'm thinking.'

Mamma had soldiers listening and watching her every evening. If she was lonely it was her own fault. Why choose the captain? She'd be better off with Oxenbury. The sooner she moved north the better. Perhaps the captain would get gassed or shot. Our family could do without Irish ferrets joining us.

'Stop worrying, Bonnie. Remember Ireland.'

What an innocent she was. Had she forgotten what happened there and the terrible death of her friend? It had happened before Tor and I joined her. She'd grown taller since then, she'd put on weight.

On our backs in a row in the big bed it felt as if we were the same age, the same size, though Ula was taller than Tor now. Why didn't Tor grow? I'd never find anyone nicer than my sisters, though Ula could be loathsome at times. She said that perhaps the captain had put an Irish spell over Mamma; the Irish could do that.

'Spells, indeed. That's rubbish. Spells are against the law.'

Mamma was not unhappy, she had no need to marry someone. Both my sisters were wrong.

Ula said that Mamma had once confided in her. She'd been miserable when Bruno died, though she'd not shown sorrow. If she'd been happy she'd want to stay with us. She didn't want to be reminded of children.

Grown-ups should never be unhappy or unreliable. They should be there when needed. They shouldn't die.

Ula said she probably didn't know what she did feel, she was muddled. She had bought the uniform and that nice watch for me.

My watch was twinkling in Clerkenwell on Red's wrist now. I had to admit that the captain had arranged this room for us beautifully. We had mauve striped curtains and mauve carpeting and the special room for our clothes. He'd asked particularly for a large room, guessing we'd like it. Our bathroom was a joy.

'I wish we had something to read.' Ula was as fond of books as Tor was, now that she could read. She liked reading aloud to prove that she did it properly, following the print with her finger. Outside in the passage was a bookcase with a row of dictionaries, which we'd never been taught how to use. There was a thin book with a brown cover, *Creatures of Myth*. Ula read the chapter headings in a loud proud voice, checking to see if we were impressed.

'The Basilisk, The Cockatrice, The Griffin, The Salamander. And The Unicorn. You see, Bonnie, they are real.'

'It's mythical, you fool. That means it's not true. It's fable, not a proved fact.'

She held up the picture of an uglier unicorn than the school one, with a longer horn and a look of contempt round the mouth.

'Read about it.'

Her singsong voice continued. ' "The other animals held the unicorn in esteem, because of its noble birth." '

'Go on.'

' "They preferred to wait until it had dipped its horn into the drinking water to ensure freedom from poison. The horn was a cure for all ills." '

'What rubbish. Anything else?'

' "If the other beasts gave chase out of envy the unicorn flung himself over a cliff in a somersault. By impaling himself on his horn the fall didn't harm him." '

'What a feeble thing to do. Any more?'

' "When the Genghis Khan invaded India he was greeted by the unicorn abasing himself so courteously that the great man reconsidered his campaign and returned with his troops, thus India was saved by a unicorn." '

'Oh *really*.'

'But listen to this part, Bonnie. "The unicorn loved to rest his head in the lap of a fair maiden so huntsmen used maidens as bait. Because the maidens loved the unicorn they protected him so the plan failed." '

'No one is going to rest their head in my lap thanks very ...'

'Oh come on, Bonnie. Play some more.'

# THIRTEEN

We were feeling hungry. When we heard noises downstairs I told my sisters to get washed and we stopped being equals. I couldn't avoid being the oldest for long. I looked at myself while I waited for them. Midge said that your glands would change. Adolescence might bring greasy skin or spots. I felt old before I'd started living properly. At least I didn't have warts round my neck or dandruffy shoulders like some Clerkenwells. One day I'd be as lovely as Mamma was with well-kept skin and hair. I would wear a long bob with a fringe dangling into my spiky eyelashes, I would drink red or green cocktails from long-stemmed glasses. I'd never desert my sisters; we needed each other. Phoebe's brother must have been suffering from war fatigue. Had they been drunk, perhaps? I hadn't smelled drink when he'd taken my hands and spoken of waltzing. War made people rude and muddled. Putting on uniforms made things go wrong.

I combed my hair flat again. Phoebe's sophistication was a veneer for her weak will. She craved attention and admiration, she was inwardly shallow. I and my sisters were deeply serious, one day we'd all be wise.

Tor's diary was still in her attaché case. I knew everything about her except what she wrote there. It was a fat little book with shiny covers and ruled lines. The first page was thickly written with two words, 'strictly private'. You could hardly see the paper under the ink. Inside the writing was even tinier. I held it close to the lamp. No margins, no punctuation, no spaces. I oughtn't to read it. I must.

*September 1939* This is a war record not about England but the way it changes things Mamma says we must to go school we went to london for our uniform Bonnie thinks clothes matter Mamma saw us in our vests when the band played at tea she had tears in her eyes Bonnie is bossy
*October 1939* The school has a unicorn Mamma was afraid to meet Miss Gee Bonnie is afraid too inside Ula and I are like Papa the other girls are silly especially Phoebe this diary is my survival I guessed Bonnie would fall in that game she got a fright when her period came
*November 1939* Bonnie goes round with Midge now Im alone I know what theyve got in the garden its a cage of mice I blame them for everything Id like to kill them Xmas will be awful . . .

I held the page closer. I couldn't believe it, not my gentle Tor. She'd known all the time about our secret. Yet she'd cried so when we'd found them, her tears had dropped on to the corpses. I would never know who had murdered them, I didn't want to know. I would love and trust Tor until death. Run in peace.

'Put that down, Bonnie. How dare you.'

She was standing in the doorway with Ula behind. Both had toothpaste on their cheeks. I'd never seen Tor look like Mamma, the same cracked dish expression, the same furious eyes.

'I was just looking, I wasn't snooping. I never knew you . . .'

'It's private. It's my diary, my own private affair.'

'I'm sorry.'

'Swear not to look again. Swear . . .'

'I'm your sister. We never have secrets, we've always told.'

'Liar. You never told about the mice.'

'That's different. I promised Midge.'

'It's not different. You're a creeping sneak.'

'What mice? What mice are you talking about?' Ula butted in. I couldn't bear Tor calling me names. She loathed me.

'Swear, Bonnie. Swear you won't do it again.'

'Yes, you'd better swear, Bonnie. Swear as a unicorn.'

'Don't be such a fool.'

'Do as Ula says. Swear.'

They made me swear on my honour as an animal of peace to obey rules of privacy. I would never touch Tor's book. I felt foolish saying it. Ula was satisfied. Tor must have enjoyed humiliating me. Were they babyish because they didn't want to grow up?

Mamma was wearing orange. She seemed to light her corner of the room. The other guests looked drab and serious, eating toast with downcast eyes.

'Can we have boiled eggs, Mamma?'

'Ula, my sweet, I've ordered fruit. You need vitamins. An apple a day keeps acne away.'

I felt ashamed of our clothes again. Mamma looked so lovely. The marmalade in the crystal jar was the exact colour of her blouse. What would the White Harte guests think of us? I peeled a green apple. Should Mamma or I write to Miss Patrice? We'd left so suddenly and she had looked so ill. Mamma was looking at Ula in disbelief, that filthy fur on her collar looked like an animal.

Ula started to explain. We had lost our clothes because the Clerkenwells preferred our uniform to their things. Mamma begged to be spared the details until she had drunk her coffee.

133

'We have nothing to wear, Mamma. There are no clothes for us anywhere.'

Then she would have to see to it, Mamma said. In the meantime did we have to talk quite so loudly at this hour of the morning? The guests were listening, though keeping their eyes on their toast. The beautiful singer had her schoolgirl daughters home for Christmas, wearing strangely tattered clothes.

'Mamma, can't I just tell you about the pageant? Bonnie and Tor were mice and goats but I pulled the Noah's ark.'

'Shut up, Ula.'

I couldn't think of the mice without a pang, without seeing their bodies lying red and torn, the worst sight I'd ever seen.

Mamma put down her table napkin. From the look of us we evidently had suffered some sort of emotional upset. She would have something to say to that headmistress, the school had not lived up to its claims. Hadn't we learned anything apart from speaking with rather common accents?

I thought of the dancing to the grammie, Barbie's thin arms winding it, I thought of the wartime songs. I thought of Midge's mouse book. A pain went through me.

I bit into my apple. I choked. Fragments of apple flew from my mouth. It was that pain again. That shooting sensation was a period. I had no one to help now, I had used up all Midge's pads.

'My sweet child, whatever is it? Is the apple sour? What a face and what a fuss.'

She wants us to look healthy, to eat fruit, to care for our looks and be a credit to her. We must speak nicely, carry ourselves well and not bother her. We are a disgrace, our clothes are disreputable. Ula has spots. Tor looks starved.

'Mamma, I have periods. I've started. I never knew.'

I bent over the green apple peel, I couldn't speak. I felt Tor's thin hand patting mine, silently comforting.

134

'How monstrous. How appalling. You mean you were not prepared?'

'How could I? I never heard of it. No one told me. No one said.'

'Didn't Gov instruct you? You mean you were not ... she didn't ...'

Tor spoke. 'Mamma, you should have told Bonnie about menstruation. You are the mother, after all. There's such a thing as motherly interest. I think Bonnie has a pain now ...'

'Period of what? Do you mean weather?' Ula dug the spoon into the marmalade. 'Don't cry any more, Bonnie. It's not your fault we lost all our clothes.'

My two sisters were defending me, braving Mamma for me. I could forgive them anything.

Then Mamma left her side of the table. She embraced me, ignoring the guests. She knelt on the floor by me, she put her face close, she rocked me back and forth like a child. She'd had no idea, she hadn't realized, could I forgive her? How remiss she had been. Come now to her bedroom with her. She'd look after me, come along now.

The room was coral pink with cream-coloured walls and overlooked the garden. Mamma pulled the curtains, she lit the gas fire, she pulled back her eiderdown. I must rest, I must stop whimpering, I was safe. She lit the lamps each side of her bed, her room was rosy. Come now, Bonnie, don't be self-indulgent. Crying was ageing, it swelled the eyelids, dried the complexion. No more self-pity. Just relax.

She opened a drawer in her wardrobe, felt under her secret underwear. There. Protection and comfort, large size, go to the bathroom.

'I'll go with her, shall I?'

'Shut up, Ula. No, you can't.'

Tor told Ula to look at the sundial outside. Remember the lawn in Ireland? We'd never seen a sundial before. Ula

135

fiddled with Mamma's dressing set, touching the silver jars and bottles. Why was Bonnie so upset?

Mamma was combing her hair when I rejoined them, examining her streak of white. She said that one day Ula would be glad of it, streaking was sophisticated. Ula stood proud and still, being praised for her appearance. Tor waited her turn to be combed.

Mamma said our clothes were like something from a bonfire night, we'd have to be fitted out again. But Bonnie darling must rest now and forget her troubles. I climbed into her wide pink bed with her hot-water bottle, I stretched down my feet with joy. Put the bottle on the stomach, she said kindly, warmth helped pain. She offered me milk with honey in it and aspirin. Her face was sweet, the aspirin was vile. I wanted the pain to stay now, she was so kind to me. I was a nasty colour, she said. Sleep a little but no more self-pity. She went downstairs to the telephone.

I was where I wanted to be, in Mamma's bedroom with my sisters perched on either side of me. They watched with grave faces. I was warm, free of pain and beloved.

'Let's see if the captain's picture is here.'

Ula couldn't sit still, she rustled about again at the dressing table, lifting the silver-backed brushes.

'Of course not. Why should it be?'

I wouldn't let a picture of that ferrety man spoil my happiness. I turned away my head.

'Behind the looking glass. Mamma hid it. He hasn't put SWALK.'

Tor looked at it too, framed in silver like Percival's, an officer's peaked cap on his head.

I would never put a picture of a man in my bedroom. Soldiers were faithless and treacherous. Had Percival really wanted to waltz with me? Had I imagined it? (Yes, oh yes. *When?*)

'Now children, darlings, everything is settled. We'll go

shopping later on. Bonnie, will you be fit enough?'

'I'm afraid not, Mamma. I didn't sleep last night.'

I closed my eyes. Did she really expect me to sit in the captain's car again while he made eyes at her? I would stay at the White Harte alone.

# FOURTEEN

'Mamma, I must talk to you. Alone, please, before you go.'

'So intense, so emotional, my sweet. Learn to take life lightly. I have had to. I assure you it's best.'

She had listened while I spoke of Tor who was too thin, too small, too sweaty and quiet. Someone must worry about my sisters. People always let you down.

She smiled in a vague way saying that children differed as much as adults. It was rare to know someone totally and completely, unless . . . .

'Unless what, Mamma?'

I had trusted Midge with our life secrets, she had told Phoebe, who had told Red.

Mamma raised her hands in protest. Midge? Phoebe? Red? Such a catalogue, spare her more please. I must learn not to be so fervent. I was getting positively overwrought. It was a great mistake to expect too much of people, she had found, particularly when you were young.

'Yes yes, I quite understand, Mamma. What exactly did Ula do in Ireland?'

Her face went stiff again, her eyes changed. A painful time. Bruno's death, a time of loss. And imagine, Bonnie, I

wasn't there for it. The shock, to arrive home ... my only
son ... .

'You were never there, Mamma.'

'How unforgiving you are. How can a child understand,
presume to judge? When your father died my interest
died. Each time I looked at you three ... .'

'You haven't got a photograph of him. Why?'

'Have you no conception, no idea of pain?'

'You never asked us if we wanted to be pushed out. To
Ireland, to that awful school.'

Her face went patchy, she started bending and pulling
her fingers like Ula. I mustn't think that she didn't want
us.

'We did think that. We think it now.'

Did she know that Tor and I had put Bruno naked under
the Christmas tree? His dangler was like a tiny snail.

'The war ... I ...'

'What about the war? You like singing, don't you? It
suits you.'

'You're so critical. Your sister Ula has more sympathy.'

'She's a baby still. She shows off. She'll probably go
mad one day. I'm not critical. I'm telling the truth.'

'Darling Bonnie, I look to you. You're my second-in-
command, my adjutant, remember? Why are you letting
me down?'

'I don't want to be any more.'

'When your Papa died, all my happiness –'

'Your happiness? What about ours? You shouldn't have
had us.'

I wanted to give her as much hurt as possible. We had
been lonely too. She'd been left without an heir, we'd had
no mother.

'You're too young to understand adult despair.'

'I'm trying to, Mamma. I'm trying.'

She said children only understood what they already
knew and had experienced. How could we understand

140

aridity of the soul?

'Aridity? Are you bored with us? What did happen to Ula? She grinds her teeth in her sleep.'

She looked shocked. Did I think Ula might have worms?

'What happened?'

'I thought you knew. She caused her friend's death in the dark. The knife in her pocket slipped, the little girl's throat was pierced. A freak accident. Imagine letting children run round with knives.'

'You never knew what we had. You weren't there.'

'Accusing me again. You are merciless!'

'I'm not. You are.'

'You liked Ireland, didn't you, Bonnie? We'll go back there, all of us, one day. You'll see.'

She couldn't help the war, she said. She had thought we were happy at school. She'd always had a singer's ambition, the army needed her.

'So did we.' I added that the uniform had been nice at first. The beautiful rust and tomato colours reminded me of mud and blood now. Clothes didn't ensure friendship or stop you feeling left out. 'And Mamma, you should have told me about ... you know ... growing up.'

She protested that she'd bought a book on sexual development.

'I didn't read it. Tor did. Tor keeps a diary.'

'Keeping diaries can be morbid. She's an introspective child.'

Had anyone tried to frighten me with old wives' tales? Had I been frightened? Did I understand everything now?

'It's not just that ... .'

'What is it, sweet child?'

I mustn't think of Red in the dormitory, mustn't think of those dreadful sounds. Those feet sticking out from the blanket, that smell like stale fish in the air. I will forget heaving bodies and dangling things. There are things I would like to know. How did the dangling thing get into you? It was too floppy. Was it pointed? Did it bleed? Probably Red knew more about bodily things than Mamma, she was more open. Mamma's face was still blotched and nervous-looking. Was she secretly afraid of intercourse?

'Are you sure there is nothing more you need to know?'

'Quite sure, thanks, Mamma.'

She looked relieved. She peered in her hand mirror, checking her mouth. I could hear my sisters in our bedroom. Ula was trying to whistle. Mamma put down her mirror. She wanted to talk about love. I must try and understand, one day I would love someone myself. Love was a blessing, you treasured it having sought it. Some women only loved once. Love, once found, stayed in the heart. It was almost holy.

'Holy? There was nothing much holy or precious when we saw it.'

'Saw? What did you see?'

My mouth felt horrid. I could nearly smell what we'd seen. My words jumbled as I tried to tell. Red and Phoebe, the look and sound. No clothes. That horrible sound. The bed. The blanket moving on the floor. The bed, the moving blanket and the sounds.

Mamma went quite white, her curls seemed to jump round her white face and staring eyes. Did I mean to say that we had actually stood and *watched*? She had put my sisters in my charge. I had let them watch like peeping cats. Why had I not gone to my headmistress? Why had I not spoken before?

'Miss Gee had died. We never mentioned it, not even to ourselves.'

Was love and sex something to praise and extol but never watch? Miss Patrice had spoken of love in the same melting way as Mamma.

She said it was quite monstrous, her own children in their own school.

142

'We were upset.'

We must put it quite out of our minds now. And believe her, love was miraculous when it was right. One day I would change, one day I would fall in love.

'I won't. I promise you I won't.' Loving my sisters was bother enough. Why should adult love be better?

'Is there anything else on your mind?'

'Why have you got a photograph of the captain if Papa meant so much to you? Why has he got one of you?'

She closed her eyes. She might have known I'd be merciless. Creeping round other people's bedrooms, prying, continually interrogating, taking her to task.

'I'm not interrogating, just asking.'

She gazed at her third finger, thinking, I expect, of another diamond ring that the captain might put there. She murmured that she was a young woman, despite widowhood. Was she allowed no second chance just because of motherhood?

'He's Irish. Look what happened to Ula there.'

'Don't be absurd. You're talking wildly. You loved Ireland, you know you did. And the captain is from the north.'

'How can you love someone with a face like that?'

Because of Ireland Ula was a manslaughterer. I was just advising, not criticizing. We were just three ordinary daughters wanting an ordinary mother, was that too much to ask? It was Christmas, better forget him and concentrate on us.

'Everything is going to be different, Bonnie, you'll see.'

'Then could you move your bedroom nearer to ours? We'd like it.'

We'd feel more like a family. We would know if she came in late. Her face lightened, she'd be delighted. Would I like to help her move her things?

I would trail back and forth with joy for her, I would carry armfuls of lovely things. I wouldn't let Ula or Tor help me. I would arrange her shoes in coloured rows. Her new room by ours had its own clothes closet, I would be queen of her castle of clothes. I would be her personal maid, her seamstress, her secretary; no one else must touch those dresses and hats. She would share our bathroom opposite her doorway. Her oils, creams and rose-smelling powders would oust our sponge and toothpaste smells. Our little tubes of cream must be put in a corner. Mamma must have all the space she required. We would wait our turn for the bathroom, we would keep watch, she must never get away. We would hear her coming and going like an ordinary mother. She would brush our hair and worry about our health.

'Look, Mamma, this petticoat is ripped. How did it happen?'

The rose-coloured satin with lace inserts was in two pieces. I will stitch it daintily to make Mamma immaculate again. She will rely on me, tell me her secrets. I will help her, she will help me. We will make merry this Christmas at the White Harte, we will wear more new pretty dresses, we'll teach Mamma dancing. The clothes we are wearing must be burned.  .

We needn't have a Christmas tree, they had brought us bad luck in the past. Our bedroom had an open fire, we would burn logs there. We would buy cards for our friends with robins, lanterns and snowmen.

'Which friends?' asked Tor quietly.

Christmas was a time of forgiving and forgetting. Should we send a card to Red? Would Midge think of me on Christmas morning, busy with presents, her pets and tree? We would make our room light and magic, with red knitted stockings to hang before the fire. We had never believed in Santa Claus. We were like three Cinderellas, our chance had come.

'Mamma, when we buy our new clothes can we go to that restaurant? We might hear Bonnie's tune.'

'What tune, sweet child?'

Ula hummed. Mamma observed that she had a sweet voice. Perhaps she would be a singer too. Acting and singing were often inherited. She smiled at her singing child. Yes, we would revisit the restaurant, and Ula must learn to eat slowly, not gollop like a little pig. How was Bonnie? Better now?

'I want to finish moving your things. I'll mend the petticoat, Mamma.' I would lie against pillows stitching, stitch her to us tight as a shadow while they went shopping. The name Mamma was old-fashioned and ridiculous. 'Mummy' was like the Magnolias, 'Mum' like the Clerkenwells.

My sisters put on those shabby overcoats. Ula was bending her knees stiff-jointedly, she was sniffing and pawing her hands. She wasn't thinking of new clothes or restaurants, she was being a unicorn.

'Goodbye, Bonnie, I wish you were coming.'

Goodbye, Tor, beloved friend. I picked up the petticoat, the busy seamstress. This time Mamma wouldn't leave us, she belonged with us. No more goodbyes. I waited until they had driven away and the road was empty. I got my coat and ran up the road again.

Our hall door was open still. I heard the clatter of the Good Companion. Oxenbury's kind dog's smile was the same.

'Hullo, Oxenbury. I've just come to ask you something.'

'Thee again, lass? What's up?'

'It's Mamma. She's too old you see, it's unsuitable. She's got us, that should be enough.'

'Too old for what?'

'She seems to have an infatuation. For ... you know ... that captain. She's too busy and she's too old.'

I was breathless. I wanted Oxenbury to agree with me. I needed support. I knew I was right.

'Too old for what?'

Illingworth was there again, with his dishcloths and tennis shoes. Kiddies on the premises again? He and Oxenbury would get cashiered.

'Cashiered? It's Mamma, Illingworth, you see. It's possible she might want to marry your captain.'

'Happen she might at that.'

Oxenbury asked how my sisters felt.

'They're too young. They don't understand. He's from Ireland, you know, the northern part.'

'We knew where he's from. He's Company Captain. Does your Mam know you feel this way?'

'She's not said anything definite. It's just that I worry.'

Oxenbury said I should tell her our feelings. Illingworth looked amused. Maybe it was a shot-gun arrangement, we'd better lump it, choose how.

'Mamma wouldn't shoot a gun at anyone, she wouldn't.'

'Don't tease her, Illingworth. Their mam could go further and fare worse.'

'She doesn't need anyone. She's got us. Don't you understand?'

Oxenbury said that life moved on, you had to let go of people. All a bit of a mystery was life.

'What do you mean?' I'd had enough of secrets and mysteries.

As Oxenbury saw it you had to let things take their chosen course. We couldn't put a rope round our mam and tie her, it would help no one.

'Well, never mind all that. The captain is quite unsuitable, apart from being from the north of Ireland.'

The captain most likely had a stately home back in the old country, Illingworth said, and able to keep the lot of us in style. He only hoped the place would be in a better state than this house had been, not a heap of rubble fit for demolition. He threw his dishtowel from hand to hand. The captain was champion. Be fair, now, wait till I knew him. I should be pleased for the sake of our mam.

I said that he never smiled or talked to us. He looked like a ferret.

'Happen he's shy of you three. Have you talked to him?'

'I've nothing to say to him, I just dislike him.' He'd never fit in with our complicated thoughts and lives.

I liked Oxenbury and Illingworth more than any men I'd met yet. They took me seriously, they were kind. They hadn't told me what I'd wanted to hear. They hadn't said that the captain was wicked, that Mamma ought to send him away. But I felt more settled and comfortable when I left them. I think they did understand.

Mamma's bed was wide and comfortable. All her things were nicely put away.

'Look, Mamma. I've finished your petticoat.'

I held it for her to see. Lovely stitching, she said, what a clever child. What a help I was going to be.

'Come into our bedroom in a minute, Bonnie. You're going to get a nice surprise.'

# FIFTEEN

I stood in the doorway of our bedroom. These strangers couldn't be my sisters, playing with a lot of toys. Our room had changed into a sort of toyshop with toys everywhere, on the floor, on the beds and chairs.

'I thought you were supposed to have been buying clothes. Have you all gone off your heads? Where are the new clothes?'

They were still in what they'd put on this morning, that be-furred blazer, that dreadful blouse. Our room was alive with stuffed animals and clockwork playthings. There was a lion almost as big as Ula, with a hectic yellow mane, a crocodile with a jointed backbone, its open mouth sharp with teeth. There was a wild-eyed mule made of leather and a family of pigs made of raffia that fitted into a basket, there were insects that flapped tin wings when you wound their tails. On the floor surrounded by more toys was Ula; she was kissing a grey velvet lamb. I had never seen her kiss anything except her gas mask. There was a high whining sound.

Tor was playing with a spinning top that flashed red, silver and gold. As it turned more slowly the humming got lower. Tor looked at me and smiled. A child's voice was singing a carol. Mamma had actually bought a gramophone. 'The stars in the bright sky looked down where he lay, the little ...'

'Oh stop, all of you. You do look silly.'

They took no notice. The child went on singing, the top went on spinning, Ula went on kissing her lamb. While I had been worrying about our future Mamma had been spending foolishly. We still had nothing to wear. I wanted to hit her; as if my sisters weren't babyish enough. I had organized her new bedroom, I had discussed her marriage future with the two soldiers. Was I the only one with any sense? You couldn't control grown-ups, you could only get attention by being ill or unpleasant, they did as they wished in the end. I had so longed for her, now I almost hated her. I wouldn't be like her when I was old.

'You are silly, Mamma. I suppose I can be thankful you didn't buy any dolls.'

There was a toy engine with wooden wheels and a chimney. There was a water pistol and a pop gun that shot a cork. Ula said she'd wanted to buy dolls. They had stopped her.

Tor plunged the spindle of the top again. The humming sound increased. The top skidded over the floor towards me.

'Do make it stop, Tor.'

The carol ended. Mamma wound the gramophone. 'Away in a manger, no crib for a bed.'

'Oh shut up, all of you.'

The three of them looked pretty and carefree in the light of the logs burning in our grate. Mamma looked as young as my sisters, all playing with Christmas toys. There was nothing woebegone about Tor and Ula now, in spite of the awful clothes. Mamma still had her fur jacket on, her collar framed her face. She took a little parcel from her pocket. Don't think she'd left me out, she'd not forget her right-hand man on such an important day. She'd bought

150

up the last toys to be found in London. Factories had to make munitions now, she'd had a spree while the going was good.

I started picking up wrapping paper. I was still angry. I ignored her little packet.

'Open it, Bonnie. I didn't buy *you* a toy.'

It was a string of seed pearls in a box with a velvet lining, nicer than anything Phoebe owned. Three turquoises were set in the clasp, blue for my eyes, Mamma said, blue the colour of hope.

'Thank you.'

'We had every intention of buying clothes and Christmas cards for your friends. We saw the toyshop, we couldn't resist. We ran out of time.'

And she had taken my sisters to the hairdresser. Ula's curls just touched her shoulders, her white lock was part of a fringe. Tor looked like a young and even thinner boy now, with dark rings round her eyes. All of us needed cheering up, Mamma said, she had done the best she could. At least she had not insulted me with games and animals. My sisters were not interested in the pearls, they were too engrossed in their toys.

'Do you feel better now, Bonnie? Let me fasten it.'

Was she pleading? Was she a little afraid? Her fingers touched my neck. Were the pearls to atone?

'While you were out I went to see Oxenbury and Illingworth.'

'Who? You mean you went home after what I said? I told you not to go there, Bonnie.'

'It's our house. Why shouldn't I? The army don't own it. We'll be going back after the war.'

'You had no right. Besides, why should you want to?'

'They're my friends. I like them.'

'You are never to go there again.'

'You do. You go there.'

'That is different. The captain is a personal friend.'

151

'Oxenbury and Illingworth are my friends.'

'That is absurd, that is entirely different.'

'Why?'

'I entertain the regiment, you know that. Apart from which, he's a family friend.'

'He's not my friend. Don't include me.'

'You are a child but you could make some effort to understand.'

'One moment I'm a child, the next moment you're giving me pearl necklaces and making me responsible for my sisters. Well I'm not a child, thanks very much. If you'd like to know, I went to ask Oxenbury and Illingworth about you and that captain.'

'You *what*? You went gossiping and sneaking to the troops about my private life? Are you out of your mind?'

'No, I'm not. I was afraid you might do something silly, something we all might regret.'

'I find it difficult to understand your lack of loyalty. Pray, what was the outcome of this top-level inquiry? What pearls of wisdom did you glean?'

She had blotches round her mouth again, her eyes were hard. Tor went on making her top hum, the child went on singing, Ula crooned to her lamb. I have made Mamma furious. I have caused her pain. I'm glad.

'Well, Bonnie?'

'They told me not to interfere. If you want to marry someone it's up to you.'

Mamma, look after us. Don't go off with that ferret man.

'For which gracious permission I'm supposed to be grateful? Perhaps you'd like me to go on my knees?'

'They quite like the captain. They admire him. They probably like you too.'

She was quiet. Had I appeased her? Mamma, I just want you to stay.

'Mamma, what is to become of us? We can't go back to that school.'

'We'll have to discuss it, naturally. It's your ... hostility. The other two are so much easier.'

'They're young.' How could we become better friends until she became more real, more of a living mother. You couldn't make things right just with a lot of toys or clothes.

'You should have come with us on the shopping trip. You are overwrought again. Fancy running behind my back and tittle-tattling.'

'I told you, I was worried, I had to tell someone. Mamma, will you be marrying that captain?'

'Don't call him "that captain". His name is ...'

'Don't tell me, I don't want to hear, I don't care what his name is.'

Her eyes were pleading again. She said I was her special daughter, she relied on me, she always had. Why must I keep probing and attacking? Couldn't I just wait and see?

'You mean I'm useful to you while you go on singing and falling in love?'

'Bonnie.'

'Do you tell Tor and Ula they're special? Do you know how they feel about anything? They might not want the captain around.'

'Bonnie, when I marry again – *if* I do, it *is* possible – you'll always be my special child. You were born first, my eldest daughter ... .'

'As if I didn't already know.'

'You could be my bridesmaid, you could walk behind me. Think of it, darling. Wouldn't you like that?'

'I was right, then. I guessed you wanted to marry him. No good will come of it, you'll see.'

'Don't say that, darling, you mustn't. This should be a happy time. I've thought it all over most carefully. It's an important decision, you mustn't be cross.'

'It's not just you, though, it's all of us.'

'I know. And a wedding would be wonderful. It's what

153

we need, a happy occasion. Something to celebrate as a family.'

'We were never a proper family.'

'We could be. A real family with a father again.'

'Would my sisters be bridesmaids?'

'I hadn't thought. They could be. I don't think so. I'd rather just have you.'

I am not like my sisters, to be bought by playthings. I don't trust flattery. What use would a father be now?

'If I did decide, what would I wear?'

'A dream dress, long and floating, don't you think? We could go to London again, just us two. We could get something made or we could try Liberty's.'

I hate your power, Mamma. I adore you. I would die for you. Will I never be free from your spell? You hurt me, you ignore me, you delight me. Must I always dance to your tune? Why should I walk behind at your wedding? I'm not your little dog to order about. I will bite your heels, I'll mess on your wedding dress. I'll howl at the people in church. Bridesmaid? Not me, thanks very much, not for a bride with dry rot of the heart.

'Let's see now. Blue for you again, I think. Blue for your eyes, blue for hope.'

There would be nothing hole and corner about this wedding, a day to remember, a pageant of love. Mamma was transported, planning, deciding. We must hurry to London again, for clothes. They might become rationed, they might disappear for ever. We might be old ladies before peace was declared. Buy now, buy and enjoy ourselves, just her and me. Oh yes and that restaurant, just her and me, we might hear my tune. It will be lovely, Bonnie, won't it?

'Will the regiment be going north?'

'Hush darling, careless talk costs lives. We mustn't discuss troop movements.' One thing she did promise, she would never leave us again. Perhaps we could attend a day school. The captain would help, he was so business-like, so fond.

'Magnolia House was miserable. I didn't ...'

'I know, darling child. Don't think of it, it's over. The important thing is I have a secret to tell. I want you to be the first to know. It's exciting.'

'What secret? What is it?' I'd had enough of secrets, I was sick of them.

'Wait and see. Wait until we go to London for our outfits. I'll tell you when we're quite alone.'

As the train left our station with Mamma and me in the first-class carriage I leaned from the window to wave to Ula and Tor. They were happy to be alone for the afternoon, they would do without me today. They pranced down the empty platform, being unicorns again. They waved their paws in the cold air, they kicked and frisked in their shabby clothes. Gas masks, deaths and separations were forgotten. Run sisters, run faster, run in peace while you can. I will never leave you, I will protect you, I will care for you. I'll teach you to waltz one day, we'll waltz by moonlight, the violins will play our tune.

'Close the window now, darling. Now, my secret.'

The train increased speed, louder, faster.

Too-old-to-dream. Too-old-to-dream. Too-old-to-dream.